WANTED!

Also by Caroline B. Cooney:
Flight #116 Is Down
Flash Fire
Emergency Room
Twins

WANTED!

CAROLINE B.
COONEY

SCHOLASTIC INC.
New York Toronto London Auckland Sydney

ISBN 0-590-98849-2

Copyright © 1997 by Caroline B. Cooney.
All rights reserved. Published by Scholastic Inc.
Point is a registered trademark of Scholastic Inc.

12 11 10 9 8 7 6 5 4 3 2   7 8 9/9 0 1 2/0
Printed in the U.S.A.   01
First Scholastic printing, July 1997

WANTED!

Chapter 1

"It's Daddy, Alice."

"Hi, Dad." Alice was a little surprised to hear his voice. He was at work in the city and rarely phoned during the day. Her eyes drifted over the Caller ID display. That was odd. It was a local number. She didn't recognize it.

"Are you home alone, Alice?"

"Yes." Of course she was home alone. She had just started spending time living with her father; she didn't know anybody on the west side of the city.

"I need you, Alice."

She was struck by his voice. It was sharp and hot.

"Get the computer disk labeled TWIN out of my top left drawer. There's a backup in the fireproof box in my closet. Get them both. Fast. Now. Then take my car and drive to — to — the place where you love to get milk shakes. I'll meet you there."

Alice was doing her nails. She stared at the three wet, finished nails and the two dry, unpainted ones on her right hand. "Dad," she said, "I don't have a license."

"It doesn't matter. Get the disks! Take the car and go! Now!"

She could hardly recognize his voice. She could not imagine what he meant when he said it didn't matter that she had no driver's license. She was putting together an argument, or at least a question, but he hung up. Even the hanging up was weird. There was a sort of violence to it, with extra breathing, as if other people were involved.

The condo was very silent.

Usually she had the radio on, but somehow in the excitement of doing her nails, she had forgotten it. Alice was a nail-biter. With great effort and self-control, she'd grown enough nail to have fake nails glued on. She wasn't used to fingernails at all, let alone long elegant nails. They kept hitting things and getting snagged on things and looking like somebody else's hand entirely. This was her first time applying polish by herself. She was right-handed and doing her left hand was fun. But it was difficult to get the polish neatly on her right hand.

Her hand felt silly, half polished, slightly smeared, hanging uselessly in the air.

Kind of like Dad's phone call.

He and Mom did share one thing: They were bears on driving technique. She had never driven without one of them. They sat on the passenger side shouting instructions, because she was always doing too much or too little of something, going too slow, getting too close, not going fast enough.

It did not look as if Alice were going to have a flair for driving.

And now her father said it didn't matter — take the car — drive away without a license.

Her father had two cars: the big Blazer, loaded with every car toy, which he drove into the city so he would be comfortable and air-conditioned and his CDs would play in a stack and he could use his car phone during the commute.

His other car was a bright red classic Corvette, the one he had dreamed of when he was a teenager.

She could not believe he was letting her touch it.

His own friends were not allowed to touch it.

Weekends, her father not only washed the car by hand, lovingly, but he dusted the interior and used Q-Tips to get the edges. It was one of the reasons for the divorce: Mom said he loved the car more than he loved her.

The whole phone call was weird.

She went to her father's office. It was the size of a closet: built-in desktop with home computer, fax, phone, and so forth. The condo was not large and everything was built-in. Alice loved it, the neatness and sharp angles of everything. Such a contrast to her mother's house, with its stuffed animals and heart stencils and lace. Alice's mother even had a mouse pad with cross-stitch patterns printed on it. It was fun to go back and forth: to live in plain gray and white at one place, and then in a riot of colors and textures in the other. Even her parents were like that: the plain father, the textured mother.

She could not put this phone call into the pattern.

4

The disk, TWIN, was in the little plastic storage box in the drawer where Dad had said it would be. Its repeat was in the fire-proof safe behind her father's shoes. She was embarrassed to be rooting around in her father's things. His neatly polished shoes and the hanging cuffs of his suit pants seemed too private to be near.

She held the disks awkwardly. She should carry them in something. But what?

The condo was on one floor. She went into the kitchen, an incredibly neat little space, with more built-ins than you could believe, but very little counter. This was okay, because Dad didn't cook. He heated things, like pork chops, and he microwaved things, like baked potatoes, but he didn't combine ingredients and stir.

She found a Ziploc sandwich bag and dropped the disks in.

She was wearing blue jeans with the knees torn out. This was done in part because both parents hated these jeans. We earn plenty of money! they would snap. Could you please dress like a person with a home instead of a person who scouts out doorways in which to sleep?

These were not clothes in which to drive a Corvette.

Alice took the disks to her room.

Her room was also small, the bed pressed up against a wall, which made it difficult to tuck in the sheets. It had just started to be okay with Mom for Alice to stay with Dad sometimes. It had just started for Mom and Dad to speak civilly to each other and not be gritting their teeth to do it. Just this month, Mom was willing to concede that Dad could have slightly different rules and standards.

Not very different. Different by a molecule.

It was hard to imagine Mom agreeing that Alice, who didn't have a license yet, could hop into the Corvette and drive across town in the midst of noontime traffic.

What had that little pause been? As if Dad had to monitor his speech? He hadn't named her destination. Said: the place where you like to get milk shakes.

It was out of town and up the river, a shack of a place, but they used local milk and cream and ice cream and made the richest, most wonderful milk shakes. Alice and Dad loved that little excursion. Salmon River Road was very curvy, and in the Vette, Alice would hang onto her seat belt and giggle like a three-year-old as Dad whiplashed the car. "You aren't allowed to drive like this," he would tell her. Alice would laugh. "Just you wait. I'm going to be a seriously dangerous driver in another week or two."

Alice didn't know how to think in miles yet. She wasn't sure how far it was to Salmon River. She wasn't sure how much time it took to get there, either. You didn't think about that when you were the passenger.

What she did think was, if she dented the Corvette Dad would kill her.

Driving the Corvette was scary. It was so long and low that your whole view of the road was different, and it had so much power. If she hit mailboxes just trying to get out of the condominium complex, she would die of embarrassment right there.

Mom's car, the one Alice usually practiced on, was a dull old Nissan Sentra: a cheap-o car for driving into the city because who cared if the radio got ripped out? One more dent would not be noticeable among all the dings and scars of city parking.

But the Vette?

One ding on the Corvette, and Alice would be the one with the scar.

She yanked off her jeans and let them lie on the floor, ripped off her T-shirt, which fell half on top of the jeans, kicked off her old sneakers, which banged into the wall and fell back onto the carpet. It was a beautiful spring day out. Alice chose a rather long, thin, cotton dress with short sleeves and a scoop neck and lots of fabric in the skirt. It was a romantic dress with tiny flowers and a pretend sash.

It wasn't a Corvette driver's outfit either. For a Corvette, Alice thought, she should have suede, and a low flat hat, a scarf, and funky earrings.

Alice considered herself in the mirror. If she kept her right hand hidden, she'd be very attractive. Alice could never decide how old she looked. Sometimes she still looked (and felt) twelve, and other times Alice was sure she could go into a bar and not get carded.

The half-polished hand felt silly. And it was her right hand, the one she used, the one she needed. Back in the kitchen, Alice got another Ziploc bag and put in nail polish and polish remover and some cotton balls so when she parked at the ice-cream shack, she could finish her nails.

She reached up for the car keys which were neatly hanging on a little brass hook above the tiny bare counter.

I don't think I should do this, thought Alice. It doesn't sound like Dad. Maybe it *wasn't* Dad. Maybe it was somebody playing a joke. What phone number was that, anyhow? I didn't recognize it. A local number, though.

Alice half thought of calling her mother for advice. But what if Mom said (and she would) "Absolutely not. I'm calling your father right this minute to demand what he is thinking! You will never stay with that man again!"

Well, that was out. Alice loved seeing more of Dad again. She had missed him terribly during the fight stages of the divorce.

Alice considered money.

She went in stages on purses. Sometimes she rejected them entirely and shoved what she needed in pockets. Sometimes she carried the whole world in an enormous tote: homework, Kleenex, pencils, calculator, books, assorted hairbrushes and lotions. Now she was copying Savoy, an annoying girl who for some reason Alice wanted to be just like. Savoy carried her laptop around. So for the last week, Alice had carried *her* laptop. The thing with laptops was, you never needed them after all, and they weighed a ton, and then their batteries ran down.

So Alice was in a purseless state.

In her room she studied the purse selection. Low. Most of her purses were at Mom's house. What kind of purse did you use for a half-fingernailed, illegal excursion in a Corvette?

Her only option was a white leather fanny pack, but she could extend the strap and use it as a shoulder bag instead.

Alice had four dollars, some change, a credit card, a PIN number, and a phone charge number. She had never successfully memorized any of these and had to carry the plastic with her.

A condo like this had two exits. There was no back door, because the back wall was shared by another unit. There was a front door in the living room and a garage door off the kitchen. She opened the garage door and there sat the Corvette, gleaming in the dark.

"Daddy," said Alice out loud, "what is going on? Why do you want me to do this? I don't want to do this. What if I wreck the Corvette? You'll kill me, and that'll wreck all my plans."

It did not steady her to hear her own voice.

In fact, she lost her breath and her heart pounded too much. Her hands got flimsy and weak, and her chin quivered.

I'll call him back, she thought. The number's still on the Caller ID display. I'll say — Dad, what is this? Some kind of test?

She stood motionless in the kitchen, and the front door of the condo opened.

Alice sagged with relief.

Dad had come home. Whatever momentary lapse of intelligence he had suffered, her father had realized that, no, Alice could not drive the Corvette, and he would have to drive.

Alice opened her mouth to yell at him, or at least to him, and a strange voice said,

"Okay, so where are these disks?"

A man's voice. Strained. Panting for air between syllables.

The door slammed and the inside bolt was shot.

Alice's heart lost its sanity and began whacking around in her chest. The little bit of air she had vanished, and suddenly it took huge scooping noisy muscular effort to fill her lungs.

Who had just come into the condo?

She could hardly hear a thing.

Was she deaf with fear, or did the thick pale carpet muffle the man's steps? Was he standing there, inside the door he'd just locked? Or was he coming toward her? He'd hear her breathe. Or she would scream in fear, and he'd hear that.

"You're a freak for neatness, buddy," said the intruder. He was panting, as if he had run to get here. "It drives everybody crazy. So those disks should be easy to find."

Were there two of them? Who was he talking to?

Nobody answered.

From near the door came a grunt. Iso-lated. It did not sound human. There was a

12

strange solid sound. Heavy. Like a couch being tipped over.

What was happening?

Alice forced herself to move silently and carefully down the two cement steps into the garage. She couldn't close the kitchen door. Like the front door, it had a very solid latch that practically clanged when you closed it.

She couldn't drive away. The automatic garage door was noisy. The Corvette was very noisy. Along the top rim of the garage door was a row of tiny windows. Alice looked out.

Whoever was in the house had backed his car into the driveway, tight against the garage door. Blocking her exit.

She saw a plain dark blue minivan, very suburban. Alice's view was restricted to its roof and rear window. Dad knew his cars by year and make, by reputation and repair record, and liked to call out identifications and give his low opinions of all other cars on the road.

The van was angled in such a way that it hid the front door — and whoever came and went — from the neighbors' eyes. Not that there were neighbors looking. Single people lived here, or working couples, and on a Wednesday at noon, nobody was home. If they were home, they weren't looking out the window, because there was nothing to see except the other side of the condo.

"Well, well," said the voice. It smirked. "Caller ID."

She could actually hear the tiny click of erasure on the Caller ID. Then she heard drawers being opened, the distinctive ball bearing sound of really good hardware. Dad's desk.

"Okay, so where are the disks?" The same voice, but angry now. High-pitched and distorted with nerves. She almost recognized it.

He won't find the disks, thought Alice. I have them. So what will he do now? And how did he get in? He must have a key; they didn't break in. The only key he could have is Dad's. How did he get Dad's key?

I'm locked in with him, Alice thought.

Footsteps. They didn't sound like two people. She was sure there was only one intruder. But — was the man talking to himself? Or to somebody else? The neatness freak had to be Dad himself. But if Dad were here, this wouldn't be happening. The man couldn't be talking to Dad.

"Clothes on the floor," said the voice. "The kid." The voice went very soft, and very threatening. The harsh whisper carried in the stillness of the condo. "You still here, kid?"

Alice turned to stone. The heart that had beat too loudly stopped beating altogether. The lungs that had sucked in air like a vacuum cleaner shut down.

What was going on?

What should she do?

There was no place to hide in the garage. The voice was correct; Dad was very neat. There was a place for everything and everything was always in its place. It was another reason for the divorce; her parents hated the way the other one kept house.

Alice had spent a great deal of time informing them that this was very shallow: A man could not leave his marriage because his wife lined the tub with twenty-seven shampoo choices, and a woman could not leave her marriage because the man said if she bought one more stuffed bunny, he was going to have a bonfire.

It turned out that Alice was wrong and people could leave their marriage over that.

If it had been Mom's garage, the football team could have hidden among the junk. Here at Dad's, Alice didn't think you could hide a jelly bean. And there was no regular door out of the garage — only the noisy automatic garage door. She could get in the Corvette, but he would see her.

Alice looked at her lovely dress and wished she had not changed her clothes. She tightened the dress around her and rolled beneath the Corvette. Inched, actually. There was not room to roll.

The Corvette was very low to the ground. But her father was too neat to permit a car to drip oil, so the cement was clean. The Corvette was very long, so lengthwise there was plenty of room.

He'd seen her clothing on the floor, but all teenagers threw their clothes on the floor all the time. It didn't mean it had happened five minutes ago.

She tugged at the skirt to make sure no flowery fabric showed. Would he come with flashlights — kneel down — tuck his neck around and look under the Corvette?

Who knew what people who broke into houses to steal disks would do?

She closed her fingers tightly around the fanny pack that held the nail polish and the two TWIN disks.

What was on those disks?

It must be very important to somebody.

Certainly very important to her father.

What did TWIN stand for? There were no twins in the family. Was it a company name? A client's logo?

Her father worked for an electronic recovery company. He spent his life retrieving lost data on computers. Usually these were accidentally deleted files or crashed systems. Every now and then it was intentional destruction by hackers. Rarely did he bring work home. Anything here in the condo was personal, and for Dad, that usually meant computer games. He loved games like Doom.

The intruder's shoes were heavy on the kitchen tile floor. The kitchen was so small he was across it in two strides and Alice knew, though she couldn't see, that he must be standing in the door. For a moment she thought she would throw up, but she'd better not; she was lying on her back and she'd drown. Alice swallowed hard.

The taste of vomit stayed in her mouth and throat, trying to get her to throw up, and the feet stayed on the step, trying to get her to reveal herself. She tightened her hands into fists to give herself courage. The fake nails dug into her palms like strangers.

The man turned on the garage light.

It was fluorescent and filled every corner.

She pictured big fingers grabbing her, and dragging her out from under the car and tearing her skin on the cement and — — and what?

She had heard only one voice, only one set of steps. And yet, the man must be speaking to somebody. Could there be two people? Was one motionless by the door? Was one tucking himself into a closet, hiding himself, so he could spring out at her?

Alice tried to remember the voice. She would have to tell the police. But she was beyond memorizing anything; she was even beyond lying here, she was so scared. She wanted to leap up and run, but she was in a tomb: concrete and black pipe and gritty underside.

She started to cry.

I can't make noise! she thought.

She forced herself to cry silently. Itchy, annoying tears ran down the sides of her face and into her hair and ears. Her nose filled but she let that run, too, because she dared not sniffle.

"I killed him good," said the voice. It was thinned out like paint, distorted with tension.

Him.

Killed *him*.

What *him* did that mean?

Not Alice's *him*. Not her father. Not that *him*.

The man turned off the garage light and the darkness was wonderful: safe and friendly. She listened. He was doing something in the house: something heavy and quick. She could not imagine what it was. She had no imagination right now — or maybe way, way too much. Her mind blotted with emptiness and then surged with the vision of a body — a him! — then hurled itself into a vision of her father, her very own beloved father — the him — killed — covered with blood, or mangled, or —

No, Alice said over and over, no.

Why had the intruder stated *I killed him good* — while standing next to Alice's hiding place? What kind of announcement was that?

At the other end of the tiny condo, the computer keyboard tapped evenly for a minute or two. It was a placid, gentle sound. Then came the shutdown music of the computer, a single sweet note.

And then the front door closed and an engine started up right next to the garage, and the minivan drove away. Alice could hear the shifting of gears, and she was surprised; hardly anybody had a manual transmission.

It was much harder to get out from under the car than it had been to get under it.

She was filthy.

She felt sick.

She was terrified.

The house seemed perfectly normal, in spite of what she had been hearing. Nothing had been touched that Alice could see. The computer was off. Nothing was out of place.

She was the only thing out of place. Her

hair and skirt and hands and face — she was disgusting.

She had to take a shower. She had to cleanse herself, not just from the filth of the car and the garage floor, but also the filth of that voice, that trespass, that terrible presence.

If she washed away the grit and the oil, she could wash away those awful words, the nightmare vision they had put in her eyes.

She bolted the front door to make sure they couldn't come back in. She should have had it bolted before. Dad would be annoyed with her. The rule was, If you're home, put on the deadbolt.

Of course, Dad might be annoyed already, because she hadn't driven to the ice-cream place. Well, she would. As soon as she was clean. Maybe she should call him right now. But what number should she call? His office, or the one on Caller ID, the one she hadn't recognized?

Dad's bathroom was behind his closet. Alice never used Dad's bathroom. She used the main bathroom, which faced the tiny center hall. She ripped off the dress and threw it in a bundle between the toilet and the door. She turned the water on high and leaped in and scoured herself, shampooing her hair twice, and all the time feeling full of electricity, little charged particles of horror and fear. What if the intruder got back in somehow while she was in the shower? What if — what if he —

She choked this back and just got clean.

She turbaned her wet hair with one towel, and togaed herself with another and ran into the bedroom for more clothes.

She dressed with amazing speed, like a crazed movie scene, whipping from one thing to another, and in the mirror she could not even tell whether she was dressed, but she felt dressed, she was pretty sure of it, and she ran back to the garage and pressed the door opener and leaped into the Corvette. It was good Dad had automatic. She remembered how he had agonized over that. Real Vette drivers shifted gears. Dad got bored shifting.

Alice shoved the key in and started the engine and inside the closed space it roared like the opening of a race. Alice's heart was doing the same. Her whole body was revving.

Alice put the Vette in reverse and took her foot off the brake and let it choose its own speed to back up. When she was out of the short driveway, and fully in the cul-de-sac, she swung the wheel much too hard — and the wrong way. She'd turned the car toward the dead end, not the exit. Alice lifted her foot in humiliation and was stranded in the tiny sunlit road.

She did not have enough breath to drive. Who would have thought driving took so much oxygen? Gasping, Alice reentered the little driveway, centered herself, and turned the wheel inside out. When she was sure she was pointed right, she gave the Vette way too much gas and hit the curb with her back tires as she shot backward.

She pressed the remote and the garage door closed slowly back down, and she found Drive, and started forward with a terrifying roar. She could hardly even see over the hood. She had to arch her back and shoulders and even then she had only a partial view of the road in front of her.

She saw somebody on the sidewalk and thought — *it's him!* —

She was so terrified she gunned the engine again, exploding out of the condominium complex. Luckily there was no traffic because she just barreled out and turned left and was off, racing, the Corvette a low red monster going for the jugular.

Chapter 2

Alice was too small for the driver's seat. Her father's legs were much longer. Alice could barely reach the brakes and the accelerator. She had to extend her legs and ankles like a new, badly balanced ballerina.

And the traffic! Trucks towered on one side, vans crunched on the other. Each red light meant gauging when to slow down, and Alice failed, braking as violently as if small children were darting in front of her.

They were not kidding about zero to sixty in five seconds. Compared to her mother's tinny little Sentra, Alice was in charge of a rocket launcher. Or it was in charge of her.

At last she was out of the city, beyond the developments, free of red lights, hurtling down the long country road toward Salmon River. No matter how slowly she drove, it felt fast. The curves tested her control. The Corvette possessed goals of its own, and if she accelerated a tiny bit, it accelerated a whole lot, and the tires screamed and left patches.

Alice was exhausted.

She was holding the steering wheel way too tightly, but it was all that balanced her, scootched up too far on the leather seat, legs extended, ankles flexed. The fake fingernails gouged her palms, as if somebody else were holding the wheel.

She could grip, steer, look, stare, tense, turn, and brake.

She could not think.

Power vibrated up through her thighs and pressed her spine back into the padded leather, but she did not take her father's joy in this. She did not have his faint smile, the one that told her he was pretending to be on a racetrack, or have the FBI on his heels.

There was the turnoff, by a low-lying meadow with a narrow glimpse of the beautiful Salmon River. The turn came quicker than Alice expected, and she took her foot off the gas late, braked late, and knew immediately that the best decision was to quit making the turn. Skip the whole thing, keep going straight, turn around later and come back. Too late for that. Alice found herself in the turn with way too much velocity. The tires screamed as if she had run over squirrels and Alice screamed, too, imagining their flat, bloody bodies, but she hung onto the wheel and missed the picket fence of somebody's yard and even got back onto her side of the road.

Thinking of squirrels had distracted her from thinking of cars. A silver Crown Victoria coming in the opposite direction had to yank into somebody's hedge to escape collision. Wonderful. The state police drove Crown Vics.

But it was no state trooper. The driver rolled his window down and leaned out to yell at her. Alice was scarlet with shame, and weak with escape. What if she had totaled Dad's Corvette?

Her mouth tasted awful, as if she'd thrown up and forgotten it.

She waved at the Crown Vic to apologize, but her fingers didn't let go of the steering wheel after all and there was no wave. She crept forward, unable to solve this, leaving the driver's furious voice behind.

There was the ice-cream shack, centered on a parking lot of broken asphalt and the kind of pebbles that lodge in shoes and tires. The place seemed to have no name, just a big brightly painted wooden cone and scoop nailed to the gable. She wondered how they had a telephone listing without a name.

She circled around the back of the shack, riding the brake. Edging up the far side meant she faced frontward and wouldn't have to back the car again.

Alice stopped.

Branches from pine trees relaxed onto the long scarlet hood. The engine would be hot, and the sap from the trees would make sticky spots hard to get off. Dad would be crazed.

But Alice could not drive another inch.

She turned the engine off and sat trembling. Waves of panic at all those near misses washed over her like ocean tides, as if now, now when she had gotten here, now she was going to drown.

It was several minutes before she was breathing like a person. She could see the road down which she'd come, and there were no dead squirrels on the pavement. That was good.

When would Dad get here? What were they going to do with two cars? She absolutely could not drive this Corvette again. She would have to drive the Blazer. No, they would have to abandon the Blazer, and somebody would have to come back for it another day, because Alice was ready to be the passenger again. Or forever.

Alice tilted the steering column, adjusted the seat, and fixed the rearview mirror. Now that she was done driving, she could see. Good job, Alice! she complimented herself sarcastically.

Only then did Alice remember the voice in her house. Herself under the car, hiding. Now a chilly ripple of fear traveled across her skin.

Driving had consumed her so completely that she in turn completely forgot what was making her drive so frantically.

Why hadn't she called the police? Why hadn't she called Dad? Why hadn't she behaved like a sensible person? So that's what panic was. It was one part stupidity, one part deafness, one part blind flight.

Chills in her bones ran down her fingers, and she found herself clenching and unclenching her fists.

And yet, the more she sat in the sun, the less likely it seemed that she, Alice, had hidden beneath a car from a vicious intruder who talked of killing. The memory dulled and became remote, like last week's television show.

Alice shoved the heavy door open and got out of the car and stood in the sun, the welcome, normal, almost-hot sun of early spring.

She slammed the door of the Corvette. The solid chunk of metal going where it belonged soothed her. Her legs held her up. They seemed to have recovered from the stretching act of the dozen miles she'd driven.

The keys were hanging from the ignition, but here in the yellow sun it seemed okay to leave them. This was a normal place for normal people. Soon Dad would be here, and he would have a normal explanation.

Alice wanted to wait for Dad before she

ordered, but she was too thirsty. She walked over to the little screened window and asked for a vanilla shake and a Coke. The Coke was handed to her right away, in a tall thin paper cup, completely different from the cups anybody else used, and that was part of the appeal; everything here had an old-time look and texture. She drank the Coke greedily, quenching her thirst, chewing on ice shards.

Through the screen she watched the boy mix that wonderful, heavy vanilla ice cream from the farm store down the road with milk from the farm itself. The world's best shake.

She paid, stuck a straw into the thick white bubbles, and sucked hard to get it to rise to her mouth. Vanilla was such a friendly flavor. A family kind of taste.

There was a strange blankness in her head, as if she had had thoughts once, and would have them again, but wasn't having them now. She could taste, and see, and be warm. But she could not think.

She went back to sit in the car and wait for her father.

He didn't come.

She had finished her shake and finished her Coke and taken both cups to the trash and still Dad had not come.

The sun made the interior of the Vette hot in a cozy, afternoon nap kind of way. By now, Alice felt proud of her drive, proud of having pulled it off, eager to boast to Dad. Maybe he drove the Vette in part because everybody else on the road was envious.

She gave the key a quarter turn for power only and the radio came on. Dad listened to the station with the best traffic reports, which did not mean the best music. Alice had always wanted to be a traffic person, leaning out the window of the helicopter, spotting wrecks, and making snide remarks about people who could not drive, and rubberneckers who made it all worse, and recognizing cars by their roofs. From a copter, Dad's Corvette would be the easiest car on the road to spot.

Alice leaned forward to tune the radio to a better station and saw her unfinished nails. She got out the polish. Its acrid, distinct smell filled the car.

The radio left off advertising and sports and moved to local news. Alice was surprised at how much time had passed. How long had it taken her to drive here? How long had she sat, mindless in the sun?

"Tragedy and mystery struck the Stratford Condominium complex earlier today," said the announcer. His voice was completely happy.

Stratford? thought Alice. That's where Dad lives.

"Thirty-nine-year-old Marc Robie was found murdered in his bedroom. Neighbors are shocked. This is the kind of place where you never dream such a thing could happen, they say."

Dad?

That Marc Robie?

Murdered in his condo?

That was impossible.

Dad had not been home.

She had been home.

Daddy? thought Alice.

"Police are looking for Mr. Robie's teenage daughter, Alice Robie, for questioning. Alice Robie was seen driving away from the condo in her father's car before police arrived at the murder scene."

Alice watched her fingers carefully screw the cap back onto the polish. She watched those same fingers open the bag, drop the polish back in and seal the plastic zipper. Her breath was not keeping her alive; she was turning blue. The plastic bag slid out of her fingers.

Murdered meant dead.

Her father.

No. She would not go along with that. It was impossible. She *needed* Daddy. She *loved* Daddy.

The reporter loved being in on the action and his voice rose several notches. "Incredibly," cried the reporter, "police were called by the murder victim's ex-wife, who received an E-mail message from their daughter Alice, confessing that she had killed her father. Alice Robie is described as five feet five inches, 115 pounds, long brown hair, brown eyes. She is driving a '94 red Corvette, license 386 JEF."

Alice wet her lips with a dry tongue. She got out of the Corvette and stumbled across the entire parking lot, suddenly a vast hideous stretch of pockmarked black and gray. Her feet and legs had not recovered from being stretched after all, because they could hardly lift themselves to travel forward. The public phone on the other side, under other pine trees, seemed as remote as another state.

Alice stared at the phone for a minute, trying to figure out its technology and what was required of her to use it. She tapped in eleven digits to get the long-distance carrier they used. Her fingernails got in the way. Then she tapped zero plus ten digits of her mother's phone number. She tapped the same number a second time, and then the four-digit PIN number so it would charge.

Tears got in her way. She could not see. She made a mistake and had to start over.

It seemed incredibly cruel, to require rows and rows of pointless mean numbers, just so she could talk to her mother.

At last it rang.

Her heart was pounding so hard she could hear it in all her pulses. Her tears were drenching her face, she was raining on herself.

"Hello?" said her mother. The voice was half scream. It had a terrible texture.

Alice loved her mother. She believed that Dad had gone on loving Mom, even though Dad had announced a million times that this was not so. But Mom had certainly not gone on loving Dad. Mom spent time in divorce support groups, which occasionally met at the house so Alice was forced to listen: ten women saying vicious things about their former husbands.

And yet Alice had gone on loving her mother just as much, and this was something Alice had not figured out: How you could love a person you thought was so wrong, wrong, wrong.

"Mommy," said Alice, and her voice broke. She clung to the heavy old-fashioned receiver of the pay phone. She wanted to cry: *Mommy, come get me; Mommy, say this isn't true; Mommy, say Daddy is fine.*

Her mother said, "Alice! Alice, the police are here! Alice, I can't believe this!" Her mother was crying. Huge wrenching sobs broke up her words. "Ally, darling, I love you. No matter what you have done, I still love you."

Alice stared at the phone. "Mom, you can't — you can't — " She could not find the end of her sentence. What had the radio said? What was Mom saying? What could it mean?

"Ally, *your father*!" Her mother's voice was a stranger's voice. "You must have been so angry! It's my fault. I should never have let you stay with him."

Alice's brain felt sticky, like the hood of the Corvette from pine sap. "Angry?" she said.

Her mother was gasping with sobs, and her voice was thready from too little air. "Oh, Alice, how are we going to get through this? Ally, I can't believe this!"

But she did believe it.

Alice moved as far away from the phone as the silver snake-metal cord would let her. She wet her lips with the same dry useless tongue. "Mom," she began, and then she had nowhere to go. Alice's brain stumbled away from her mother's words.

Her mother regained some control. With a tremendous effort, she whispered, "Where are you, honey? You be a brave girl. I love you. The police and I will come for you."

Alice pulled herself together. "Mom, what are you talking about? I didn't do anything. There was this man. I never saw him — actually, I was hiding — and Dad wasn't even there. I don't know what message you're talking about, but —"

"Alice, the police are on the phone, too. I don't want you to say one more word until we have lawyers. We're not going to make up stories about strange men. We're going to tell the truth. I mean, Ally, we have your confession!" Her mother was sobbing again, but talking through it, as if she were two people. "Just tell me where you are, Alice, so that we can come and get you."

Alice hung up.

She walked back to the car. She got in. Shut the heavy door.

Through the open window she listened to the river flowing over rocks. It was a peaceful, eternal sound.

Alice started the engine. It was not peaceful. People own Corvettes in order to disrupt the peace. Alice checked for traffic, dogs, and bikes. Drove away.

It was easier this time. The seat back supported her now, and her feet rested against the pedals, her heels correctly on the floor of the car. Memory of wrong decisions had stayed in her hands and feet, and she drove properly now, exactly centered on her side of the road, without problems at curves and stop signs. She was even getting used to the fingernails.

She had never driven any further down this road. She and Dad always ordered ice cream, turned around, and went home.

Here the road bordered Salmon River, and on her right the stream was wide and shallow and twinkly. There wasn't much countryside left in this part of the world. In a few miles she was back among houses again, and then abruptly, on the edge of another city. The road got wider, and went from two lanes to four, and from four to six, and there were strip malls and superstores and factories and warehouses and Alice did not know where she was.

She was weeping.

For a moment the tears were so heavy and thick they were like gelatin, and she could not see, but the car was well-balanced and stayed on course, even when she took a hand off the steering wheel to wipe her eyes. She came to an entrance of a parkway.

The name of the parkway was familiar, but Alice had not done enough driving to learn the geography of her own state. She did not know where the parkway went.

It occurred to her that it did not matter where it went.

If Dad was dead — and she did not believe it. She could not have that be true; plus, Dad *had not been there* in order to be dead! Well, but if he was, then she did not have that plain gray-and-white tailored home anymore. And if Mom really believed that her only daughter, her only child, her Alice, her baby, was capable of killing somebody — and not just anybody, but Dad, whom Alice had defended through a million fights and arguments — then Alice did not have a home with Mom either.

Alice turned onto a ramp. East, it said. Alice truly did not know whether her own city was north, east, south, or west of where she was right now. But east felt distant, it felt like a going-away direction, not a going-to direction, and Alice merged with traffic, which was simply luck. She could not seem to turn her head to look for a space, nor use the side mirror. Her neck was a wooden post.

We already have your confession. Confession of what? How could Alice have confessed anything? How could Mom believe it?

It was harder than she had expected to keep her speed steady. Her foot played with the accelerator, trying to learn the right amount of pressure, but the trouble was, going uphill or downhill or on the flat required different amounts of pressure.

I killed him good, the almost-familiar voice had muttered.

What did "good" mean in that context? Thoroughly? Or with pleasure?

Alice needed cruise control. She could see buttons and dials with words on them, but she could not read. Was she crying too hard? Or could shock shut down the reading segment of your brain?

People admired the Corvette. As she passed them, or they passed her, their eyes floated down the slick scarlet body of this sexy car, and in each case they were startled to see her. She was the wrong driver for such a car, and everybody knew it.

And Alice thought: They announced my license plate over the radio.

Chapter 3

They had announced her license plate and described her car.

Alice had so much to think about, she could think about nothing at all. Was she a fugitive from the police?

She, Alice.

Tenth grade. Taking American literature, and physics. French Two and Algebra Two. American history. Chorus and gym.

She, Alice.

A nice pleasant girl who didn't butt in line, didn't write graffiti on the bathroom stall doors, didn't drop her hamburger wrapper out the car window, didn't cut pages from library reference books.

The police, the radio announcer, *and her very own mother* believed she had committed a murder.

The murder of her very own father.

The red Corvette was a splendid decoration on the road. Nobody could miss it.

How many people who admired her Vette were listening to the radio right now? Had the boy in the ice-cream shack been listening to the radio? Who, speeding down the parkway, had a car phone? Dad's Blazer had a car phone, but he didn't keep one in the Corvette. The Vette, he said, was for escape.

Dad had a daydream he liked to use when he drove the Vette — that he was escaping. Running. Keeping pursuit off his tail. "Look back," he used to say when she was little, "recognize any of those cars? That white sedan, the one with the tinted windows — it's following us! Here. We'll leave 'em in the dust." Alice and Daddy would holler joyfully while they left 'em in the dust.

Then Mom, who had loved this game for years, suddenly said it was childish and dangerous and stupid.

Alice wanted to shove the accelerator to the floor, drive two hundred miles an hour, put dirt and towns and mileage between herself and the phone call to her mother. This was the car to do it in.

I can go eighty. In a Vette, I can do ninety. A hundred. That's what it's for.

But this was not a good time to get a traffic ticket.

She let a glitter-beige Avenger pass her. Dad would never have permitted such a thing. Corvettes do not get passed; they do the passing. Dad loved the name of that car — *Avenger* — but not the handling. Dad had always wanted to be a car namer. Dodge Ram, he would say. Great name. Great truck.

Coming toward Alice, cut off by the scenic divider, was a police car. Its lights and sirens were on. It hurtled forward. The sound of its siren was heart-slicing. The lights ripping around in circles were the lights of hell, of jail, of torment.

The lights of your very own mother believing quite easily that you, her only child — you were capable of killing your father.

Mommy, thought Alice, *how could you?*

Her mother was a pretty woman, but not beautiful; a little chubby; fond of jewelry, always changing her hairstyle, always on the phone with her friends. Her mother loved to cook. Loved to decorate. She worked in the city for a firm that designed mail-order catalogs. It was a job that fascinated her, and she could never resist the useless but beautiful objects sold in the catalogs she designed.

Alice drove faster. The Corvette turned human, and let her know that it loved speed; it yearned for speed. Alice held harder to the steering wheel, to be sure *she* made the decisions, not the Vette.

The cop was in the left, faster lane of his side. When he saw the Corvette, he slowed.

There was no doubt about it. He slowed.

For a moment they were suspended across from each other. Alice, who had been going 75, easing off, and the cop, who had been going even faster, easing off, too, looking her way.

Their eyes did not actually meet, because they were too far apart and because Alice had lost the ability to focus her eyes. But she knew he had spotted her; he was going to get to her side of the parkway and come after her.

He could not cross here, but within a quarter mile, a half mile at the most, the police car could find a spot to bump up onto the grass, squeeze between trees and rocks, and come after her.

Alice was sobbing, but they were dry sobs. It was more that her heart and lungs were yelling. Her hands got so cold and slippery she could barely hold the wheel.

For a moment she considered just pulling over, letting him come, telling him what had happened, explaining that her father had *told* her to drive the Corvette, that she was bringing Dad the computer disk, that —

No. She was not bringing him anything. He was dead.

The parkway blurred; she felt like a small child in need of glasses, confused by a world of color smudges.

If all she had to do was talk to a policeman, Alice could stop the car. But talk to Mom? Who had just said: *We're not going to make up stories. We have your confession.*

Mom had been talking of getting married again (she who had bungled the only marriage that mattered. Dad protested vigorously that his daughter should never have a stepfather. Mom and Dad had talked of going to court in a custody fight, but they couldn't; Alice was too old; she could decide; and she had decided they had to stop their nonsense and share their daughter better.

Alice imagined Mom's friend showing up at the house right now. Her mother called him Rick darling. Alice never called him anything. Alice made a point of never meeting Rick's eyes; facing away from him when she was forced to speak to him; having urgent social activities whenever there was a threat that Rick might be present for more than half a minute.

Alice imagined Rick saying, "Chrissie, we must stand by your daughter. Whatever dreadful things she has done, we must be brave and remain at her side." Alice heard her mother saying, "Rick darling, I'm so glad you're here; what would I do without you?"

Her father saying (because he *was* alive after all, and had a voice, and a heart, and loved Alice), "Come on, sweetie, give me a hug; everything's okay. I'm here; it'll work out."

Thinking about her parents was so painful and hideous, a great black vortex that might suck her down and leave her insane, Alice decided not to think about either of them. She would think car thoughts.

An exit sign loomed.

Alice got off the parkway.

She had absolutely no idea where she was, and she had to hide from the police while driving (badly) the world's most obvious car.

She'd gotten off at the kind of road with stoplights every quarter mile. Endless strips of stores and parking lots and — and a mall.

Westtown Mall. A mall she knew well. It was a mere five miles from her mother's house. Alice had not driven away. She had driven right back. There was no time to yell at herself for such stupidity. It had happened. She must deal.

The mall was an immense array of white buildings one, two, and three stories high, sitting in the midst of a truly vast parking lot.

There was not just outdoor parking. There was underground parking. Alice found the entrance and coasted down the ramp, between huge scary cement pillars, and into a damp, dark world with dim lights and cars creeping out of corners.

She needed headlights but could not remember how to turn them on. She needed both hands on the wheel. The horrible sick feeling in her stomach threatened to leap up and fill her throat and mouth.

She braked at the same time she gave it gas, goosing the car in a jerky, incompetent sort of way. People who owned Corvettes were terrific drivers who loved driving, and now in this hideous cellar for cars she would end up burying her father's beloved Corvette.

Could it be true? Would Dad never sit behind this wheel again, never play footsie with the state cop radar, never pride himself on how he drove way above the speed limit without getting caught?

There.

Two spaces next to each other.

Alice measured the space with her eye, trying to match it against the long front end of the Vette. Prayed. Turned. Braked.

Halfway into the slot, a cement pylon pressed up against the front bumper. The perspective must be confusing her. Other cars fit, and hers was not in fact six feet longer. It just felt that way. A mistake would smash up Dad's car. She must not make a mistake.

Confession, she thought dimly. What confession? E-mail. What E-mail?

Alice inched forward until it seemed the cement pylon must be in the front seat with her. Finally she was even with the car on her left and surely that was good enough. She yanked up the parking brake. She turned off the ignition. Lifted her tired right foot from the gas. Rested her feet flat on the floor, folded her arms on the wheel as if on a pillow, and put her cheek on her arms.

The car sat silent and dark.

Alice did E-mail her parents constantly. It was easier for them at work than the telephone, and it was fun. She could comment on the dumbest or most profound parts of her day and her thoughts; she could slip into the school library at lunch and say Hi; she could be at the other parent's house, and call in. She loved E-mail.

Today she had not sent a message to either parent.

Alice struggled to focus.

Okay, she could make no sense of the

reference to E-mail. But the disk Dad had so urgently required must have something to do with his work. Dad had access to all kinds of classified information at major corporations. That was his job — getting it back for them, or protecting it in the first place. Had Dad uncovered something he shouldn't know? Had he found out something about a person or a company they didn't want found out?

But why bring the disk home? Surely he would just show it to Mr. Austin or Mr. Scote, who owned the company, and it would be their problem.

A freak for neatness, the man's voice had said. Drives everybody crazy with it.

So this voice must work with Dad. Must have been driven crazy. And Alice had almost known the voice, so it was a person she almost knew, too. Alice had met few of her father's colleagues, and Mr. Scote and Mr. Austin only a handful of times.

If Dad had actually been killed, which was impossible, Alice would not accept this idea, but if he had, that voice had done it. Done it where? At that phone number? The one on the Caller ID display? Or in the condo? While Alice lay beneath the Corvette?

This, too, was impossible.

Alice massaged her arms and wrists, trying to press down the tremors that assaulted her.

Okay, the Corvette was parked, she'd lost the cop; now what? She had to phone her mother again. Finish that conversation. Everything had gone wrong in that crazy sobbing minute over the phone. This time Alice would ask the right questions and state the right facts.

A car slid silently into the space next to her. It was spooky and awful, the way its engine was so quiet.

It was a van.

Her heart slammed. Her fingers iced.

No. It was not *that* van, which had been navy blue. This was a Windstar, in one of the crayon colors popular this year, driven by a very large woman who was finishing her cigarette as she heaved herself from the van. She reached back in to grind out the cigarette and then gathered an immense purse and a shopping bag from Macy's department store.

Alice thought: She's returning something and she's in a bad mood about it.

The woman squeezed between her car

and Alice's and headed for the mall entrance, and now Alice thought: She left her keys in the ignition.

Keys.

Ignition.

If Alice could not drive the Corvette, because the police were searching for it . . . *could she drive another car?*

The woman vanished into the mall. There would be telephones in the mall. Should Alice find a phone, or drive away?

Alice needed time to think. She could not shake off her shock and confusion. Maybe she should drive away . . . in somebody else's car. One with the keys conveniently hanging from the ignition.

Could she just get out of the Corvette, climb into the van, and drive off?

Alice had never stolen anything in her life. Not a pack of gum. Not even a pencil off a teacher's desk.

Alice got out of the Corvette and locked it. Dad never parked in places like this. He parked way at the back of lots, a hike from the mall entrance, angling the Vette over two spaces so nobody could open a door and dent his beloved car.

Alice looked into the Windstar.

She was right.

The vehicle was not locked. The keys were there. The car was hers to steal.

Alice stood with her nose pressed against the van window, like a child staring at toys.

A few hours ago I was worried about whether I could get the nail polish to lie smoothly on my fake nails, thought Alice. Now I am considering whether to steal a car.

She thought of her best friend Kelsey. She and Kelsey had managed the exact same class schedule for two years, and were co-captains of JV softball. Kelsey would never believe that Alice could behave like this. Alice, who never even pretended to be sick in order to miss a test? Evading police and stealing cars?

The rest of her friends — Emma, Laura, Cindy, Mardee — would think: Alice? She doesn't even ask the office to let her switch teachers when she gets one she can't stand. She's not going to kill somebody. Certainly not her own father.

Then they would think: *but it does happen.* Look at that woman who drowned her two little boys.

All right, said Alice to herself, talking to Mom comes first. I have to get to a phone. Besides, if I take the van, where would I drive? I have to have a destination. The only destination I've ever had is our house, which is now just Mom's — probably Rick darling is there. Probably police — probably even police in my bedroom — touching my things — looking for clues!

At her father's condo, there must also be police. And reporters, obviously. TV cameras, and —

Alice shut her mind down like a bank at night, refusing to think of where and what Dad might be.

So far, she thought, the only thing I've done wrong is to drive my own father's car without a license. I can get into trouble for that, but I don't think a whole lot of trouble. Do I want to add car theft? Do I want that woman, who's angry anyway over her package, to come back and there's no van here?

In the creepy way of headlights in the dark, the lights of a car not yet visible made jumping rectangular patterns around the rough cement walls of the parking garage.

Alice thought: It's the police car.

She'd been hanging out as if she had all the time in the world. Things to analyze, strategies to plan, anger to feel. But if those headlights belonged to the cop, she had no time at all.

She thought of hiding in the van, hunching down —

— but that was childish and ridiculous, like hiding in your own closet if you heard noises.

The police would be all over the Corvette in seconds, and she would be trapped inches away.

That is stupid, thought Alice. I am stupid. This is what you are supposed to learn from all these years of watching television. Cooperate with the police. Tell the truth. Be a good girl.

Alice had definitely watched her share of television. She and Dad were partial to real-life cop shows and always hoped that for once, instead of filming in Atlanta or Los Angeles or Miami, they'd come here and film streets Dad and Alice would recognize.

But a girl whose very own mother believes she is capable of murder . . . police who have a confession . . .

Alice reminded herself that forensics was a very advanced science. The pathologist would establish that Dad had not been killed in the condo. Couldn't have been.

Alice's face twitched, as if she had tasted something awful, and could flinch off the disgusting flavor with muscle spasms.

It was imperative to get away, take the disks and read them, find out what was on them, do something more sensible than steal a van. Maybe — maybe — maybe *what*? There were too many choices and no choices.

The lights of the approaching car cast quickly changing shadows across her face.

It occurred to her that maybe Dad had *not* been killed someplace else.

Maybe the man had brought a *living* Dad into his own bedroom *and killed him there*. Maybe that was the inhuman groan she had heard.

Alice's own inhuman moan whimpered out of her mouth. She stifled it, and panted tiny shallow breaths, like a desperate dog.

Alice decided to do what any girl would do in a similar situation.

Shop.

Chapter 4

Alice ran between the rows of cars, following the direction the fat woman had taken. The underground mall entrance was small and dark, without the gleaming two-story pillars of the main entrances.

Should I look back? Alice wondered. Letting her eyes move in the Corvette's direction would show her face to the policeman, like a deer caught in the headlights. But she had to know.

The door rotated automatically, letting one person enter at a time, so Alice could not linger on the threshold, considering things. Yanking her long hair out of her eyes, Alice looked fast over one shoulder, and there, partially visible among cement pillars, was a police car.

Alice stepped into the mall. Instantly she was part of a swirling crowd of anonymous people. Wednesday must be a big shopping day. Nobody looked at her, because nobody cared. They cared about themselves and their purchases.

The door had led Alice into the downstairs area of a low-end department store, among appliances and hardware. It amazed her to see couples stroking washing machines, women opening vegetable drawers in refrigerators, men examining the gears on yard tractors. It was so normal. She wanted to explain to these people that nothing was normal now.

A scream was sitting inside her, waiting to leave. If she let go of her control for a single second, the scream would barrel out with as much force as the Corvette. Alice fastened her jaws together hard enough to break fillings.

She found the escalator with the ease of a practiced mall-woman and went to Clothing on the second floor. She moved swiftly among the racks, getting a pair of generic jeans, a pale pink T-shirt size L, the cheapest sneakers in the world, which would probably fall apart in an hour, and from a bin of generic baseball-style caps, grabbed the one on top. There was a vertical rack of sunglasses, and old-people reading glasses, the kind where you didn't go to the eye doctor first, and Alice chose a pair with nerd rims, wide and black.

She didn't try anything on.

She didn't insist on brand names.

She didn't even read the logo on the cap.

There was a line at the cash register, and this time Alice did not let herself look around, nor think of police, but stayed close to a woman her mother's age, as if they were together. Her charge card startled her. When she signed the sales slip, she thought: This is a paper trail. I am leaving a trail.

The mall was a vast T, with soaring ceilings, and anchor stores at the ends of the cross. There were ledges and seats and perches, three-story strips of hanging ivy, odd little wagons for crystal earrings or photos printed on T-shirts. There were families and strollers and canes, there were sweats and high heels and flapping sandals.

A jutting balcony, as large as a gym, was filled with tiny food shops: chocolate, french fries, Orange Julius, tacos. A semicircle of public telephones stood at one side, each phone fastened to a high gleaming steel pillar.

I have no idea what I am doing, thought Alice. Why am I buying clothes? I have two walk-in closets full of clothes at home!

She moved toward the phones, thinking: My mother loves me. She's a sensible woman and I'm a sensible daughter. One phone call, and we'll clear this up.

All six phones were being used.

Alice listened to each conversation, trying to figure out who was likely to stop first. At a time when Alice so urgently needed to speak to her mother, the conversations these strangers were having were stupid and worthless.

Two security guards, each talking into his hand phone, came jogging down the hall.

Me, thought Alice. Those men are after me. The police alerted mall security.

It had been terrible to see the car that had chased her, but to see the actual men . . . see their faces, and hands, and weapons (*weapons!*) and know that they were taller and stronger . . . that their actual job, their actual assignment, was to catch Alice . . .

All the security staff need do was close the mall exits. So it was necessary to leave before that happened. Forget changing clothing.

In fact, now that Alice thought about it, how could they know what she was wearing? It was the car that had been described, not her clothes. She had wasted precious time getting an outfit that would blend in. She had forgotten the important thing — she had to get away.

Alice slipped around knots of shoppers and walked swiftly into the department store from which the security men had come. She went through Perfume, its glass counters sparkling with bottles, and through Handbags, leather and cloth and designer — and there was an exit. Two automatic doors, flanked by two push doors.

A security guard was standing there, facing into the store. He was not lounging. He stood solidly, legs spread, arms folded. His eyes shot around, little scouts in the wilderness, *hunting for her.*

Alice took a handbag from the display and tore off the price tags as she walked through Lingerie over to Swimsuits. She pushed through the cash register line, annoying shoppers, and held up the purse to the overworked, exhausted clerk. "Someone left her purse in the ladies' room," she said. "Would you please call Security to come and get it?"

The clerk beamed. "Oh, how nice of you!" The women in line softened. Today's young people were not so worthless after all.

Alice smiled back. This was too bad. The clerk and customers were going to be able to describe her and her clothes. Alice set the handbag on the counter, hoping nobody would go through it just yet, since the only contents were smushed store paper to keep the bag from sagging.

The clerk picked up her phone.

Alice walked back, taking a route behind racks full of clothes, and sure enough, frowning, the security guard headed toward Swimsuits. He walked sideways, keeping an eye on the door.

Alice crouched between tightly packed nightgowns and shimmering satin robes. Stooped over, she got as close to the exit as she could, straightened up, shoved the door open, and ran.

Flew, actually.

Her skirt and hair lifted behind her, and her shopping bag and purse whapped into cars as she raced past them.

She had visualized the parking lot as an easy place to hide, a thousand cars behind which she could duck, but she was taller than the cars. She was completely visible.

And there was no place to go. At the far side of the immense lot was the six-lane road she'd driven off of. Not the sort of road you easily crossed on foot. There was nothing on the other side but more stores, more parking lots, more exposed places where pedestrians did not hang out.

Halfway across the lot Alice knew she was ruined. Running away was one thing, but you had to have somewhere to end up.

I have nowhere to end up, thought Alice.

She heard a yell from the mall. "Hey! You!" It was a big, chesty, masculine yell. An authority yell.

A truck backed out almost on top of her. Alice had to brake as if she were a car.

It was a Ford pickup, not the cute little suburban kind, but a big solid V-8 work truck. It was not new, and the back was filled with stuff. A tarp, a barrel, some tools, a ladder, several cement blocks, empty white buckets. The tailgate was gone.

The driver could not see behind him. His interior rearview mirror was blocked and he was backing in that slow way of people who are hoping immovable objects will move out of the way.

Alice threw her purse and shopping bag behind the cement blocks, put her two hands on the bed of the truck, and jumped in. Turning on her fanny, she pulled up her feet and skirt, crawled up against the junk and yanked the tarp over herself.

The truck changed gears painfully and slowly. Then even more slowly, it drove forward. Had the driver seen her get in his truck? Had the security guard seen? Was any of this really happening, or had her imagination split like an atom, causing a bomb of made-up nightmares?

The tarp was brilliant blue plastic, very thin. She felt outlined. The truck bed was filthy with spilled oil, paint, gunk, and food wrappers.

The truck turned, and turned again. Were they heading out of the mall or toward the guard?

The truck lurched and then leaped out

into traffic, the driver ramming through gears as if he were hours late for the most important event of the year. Alice braced herself on the corrugated floor of the truck. They drove for a minute and stopped dead. Alice and the junk tipped, and then fell back in place. They must have hit a red light.

When this had happened twice more, Alice took the tarp off. Her truck was in the third, interior lane, completely surrounded by cars and vans and other trucks. A very curious driver in a Mazda was watching Alice.

She twinkled her fingers at him and he grinned, surprised and interested, and waved back.

The light changed, and this time Alice's truck drove straight for perhaps a mile. Buildings emerged from the wrong direction, because she was sitting backward. She saw every fast food chain in America — Dunkin' Donuts and Taco Bell and Ruby Tuesday's and Burger King. It made her hungry even while the thought of food also made her sick.

At each red light, Alice told herself to get off.

But it was dangerous. Right here in the midst of vehicles and idling engines and turning trucks? Just slide off hoping nobody would run her over? Dart through several lanes of traffic?

Alice was not a danger-seeking kind of person. She used seat belts. She put water-proofing on her winter boots. When she did homework on the computer, she always made a backup.

It was too late, anyhow. Abruptly, they left the city behind and were among large yards and houses set way back off the road.

Alice tried to think through the geography of this. Westtown Mall was about five miles from Mom's house, and about five miles the other direction from the city itself. She wasn't familiar with this road, so were they heading back out to the country? Or was this a diagonal, and merely another way through the suburbs that ringed the city?

Now there was nobody behind them, and Alice had time to be afraid of the driver of her truck. The driver she had not seen; did not know the gender or age of. What would he/she do about Alice when the drive was over? Where would they be? What would Alice do?

Her brain was capable of questions, but not answers.

When the truck stopped again, Alice hung onto her plastic shopping bag and her purse, scooted to the edge of the truck, and slid off. She walked away, trying to look like a person who had been on the edge of the road all along.

The light changed. The Ford moved on.

She could not stop herself from checking. She turned and looked, and incredibly, the driver's hand was sticking out of the window, waving at her.

She could not wave back. It was too casual.

Had it been a teenager, delighted to have a sudden hitchhiker? A mason or a housepainter, amused by some weird girl's antics? A shoplifter, willing to bail out a fellow criminal?

The truck disappeared around a curve, and Alice was alone.

Ordinary houses looked like fortresses.

Garage doors looked like traps and small dogs like Dobermans.

Alice tried to walk as if she belonged here and knew where she was going. Anxiety turned to crippling fear, and now her ankles hurt, and her knees, and hip joints, and spine, and she wanted to lie down on something soft, and curl up, and pull a blanket over her face, and then have Dad kiss her awake from her nap and her nightmare.

What am I doing? she thought. What do I do next? I need help.

The only person who could explain this horror was Mom.

What if explaining was not enough? What if, after Mom finished explaining to the police, they still thought Alice had killed her very own father?

Every house she walked by must have a telephone, or two or three or four. She actually thought of breaking into a house just to use their phone; explaining to whoever was sitting there, This is an emergency.

A yellow sign warned oncoming cars to be careful of children crossing the street. Alice crossed in the crosswalk, to establish how law-abiding she was. How filthy the back of her dress must be. The dress was cream with scattered tiny red and black flowers, a vaguely Persian pattern. She felt extremely visible.

Around the corner was an elementary school, named for a person, probably a local heroine. Margaret P. Trask School, it said.

Alice's school had a day off. A professional day, during which teachers were supposed to be learning a ton of useful stuff and you got to stay home, learning how to use nail polish. But this school must be in another district, because it was open. Playing fields stretched on three sides of the school, and kids were struggling with various forms of baseball and T-ball. School must be almost over; empty yellow buses had begun to line up.

Alice was not wearing a watch. Was it two in the afternoon? Three? When had Dad phoned? Eleven? It seemed to Alice that she had a commitment this afternoon. What was it?

This did not seem the time to worry about whether she had a dentist appointment or had promised to call Kelsey.

If Alice had ever needed a best friend, it was now. But Mom would have phoned

Kelsey to see if Alice had gone there. The police would be asking Kelsey to guess where Alice was.

What guess would Kelsey make? Would Kelsey tell the police anything? Would she believe for a single instant that Alice — who had spent the night with Kelsey a million times, and shared pizza, and rented movies, and popped popcorn, and most of all discussed boys, boys, and still more boys — was a killer? Whose side would Kelsey be on?

My own mother is not on my side, thought Alice.

A class bolted out a side door of Margaret P. Trask, scattering over the grass. Their teacher clapped her hands. Her students were like little magnet filings, coming back to her. "Hi, how are you?" Alice said to the teacher. Alice smiled at the class, and went in where they had come out. It felt very schoolish in here, with light tan tiles, and art papers on the walls, and the sounds of chatter and chalk coming out the doors.

She was walking toward the front of the building, toward the principal's office, where phones would be, when she remembered that in elementary school, you had to ask to use a phone. Phones were behind the secretary's desk. Or in the nurse's room. They were not lined up, mall-style, in the hallways. How could she use a phone here, considering the conversation she expected to have?

She walked past two closed doors, two open classroom doors, and came to a Girls' Room.

Inside, the toilets were tiny, and the sinks very low.

She stepped in a stall and changed into her new jeans and T-shirt. She had no way to cut the tags and had to rip them off. It tore a hole in the shirt. Alice had plenty of T-shirts with holes, but this hole seemed too much and once again she had to battle tears. She took off her sandals and yanked on the new sneakers. They, too, had to be torn to separate them. She made a ponytail of her long hair, threaded it through the hole in the back of the baseball cap, and tugged the visor low on her forehead.

Her face puckered like a lemon, and then, horribly, her stomach, too. Alice whirled, bent, and threw up very neatly into the tiny toilet. She stayed clutching the white porcelain sides while her stomach and her face settled back into position, and then it was over.

You can fool your mind, she thought, but not your gut.

The awful quick animal panting returned for a minute and then Alice forced herself to the sink, washed her face and mouth and teeth with her hands, shoved her old clothes back into the shopping bag, slung her purse over her shoulder, and headed out the way she had come.

One class had left book bags outside their door.

There were movie character book bags: Pocahontas and 101 Dalmatians. There were teddy bear book bags and L.L. Bean book bags, tiny second-grade-sized book bags, and huge Dad-goes-camping backpacks.

Alice did not even pause. She picked up a Dad-goes-camping, slung the backpack over her shoulders, and headed on out. There. She had committed her first crime.

It horrified her. She had to escape this place, this innocent stretch of hall, where she had become a thief. Alice dropped the shopping bag and fanny purse in among some poor kid's chapter book, forgotten permission slip, and the remains of a snack.

She ran.

The running felt wonderful. Alice always felt thin and athletic in jeans, as if she had longer legs and a better personality. She loved any sport with a run. In softball, she was always sorry the bases weren't farther apart.

The slamming of her feet felt useful, as if she were accomplishing something. She liked the speed at which she put distance between herself and Margaret P. Trask. Running was good because it replaced thought, and Alice had not been doing well on the thought front.

Alice ran about a mile, and then got hit by exhaustion as if by a train. All at once she could not even lift her feet, and her shoulders trembled under the weight of the backpack, whose wide padded ribs kept falling off. Her throat burned where she had thrown up.

The tears spilled again.

Stealing a little kid's book bag. It was disgusting. It was the most low-life thing Alice had ever done. She would have preferred to get caught stealing the Windstar.

How could she make up for it? How could she ever explain what made her decide to do it?

It was nothing, it was minor, anybody in her position would do it, she told herself.

But nobody had ever been in her position before, had they? Did this happen to other high school sophomores?

Alice walked facing traffic, but not really, because she was keeping her chin down and her eyes on the pavement. She reminded herself that she looked exactly like a million teenagers; nobody could tell she was Alice, nobody would stop and ask.

Please don't hit me, she said silently to the cars she was not looking at.

But somebody had hit her father. Hit in the television series manner: *killed. I killed him good.* How could that have happened to her father?

Dad hadn't been at Austin & Scote very long. He changed jobs a lot. He was so good at what he did that he kept getting offers he couldn't refuse.

Alice could vaguely picture Mr. Austin and Mr. Scote. Middle-aged, going gray, and going bald. She remembered their cars, of course: a stunning silver Jaguar and a black Mercedes that looked like part of a presidential cavalcade.

Would Mr. Austin or Mr. Scote recognize Alice? Did Daddy keep a photograph of Alice on his desk? But it didn't matter, because Austin & Scote was not a place where Alice could slip in unnoticed and riffle through the papers on her father's desk, or open up his computer files to see who his enemies were.

The company was high-security: You had to have a photo ID to get into the building, and Austin & Scote had their own elevator, run by a uniformed person, not buttons. If you didn't have a pass, you didn't go up.

Alice could not get into Dad's office to find out anything, and in any case, she had not the slightest idea what to look for, nor how to look.

Dad enjoyed his work, but that did not mean his co-workers were honest. These men and women had access to corporate plans, strategies, patents, formulae, sales figures, mailing lists. Suppose there was more money in selling these secrets than in protecting them?

Suppose that *Dad* had a secret to sell and —

No.

Alice refused to think even for a moment that Dad was the one doing something wrong.

She had to get to a computer and read what was on the disk that mattered so much.

She plodded on. The buildings ceased to be houses and became doctors' offices. Accountants and lawyers. And then, blessedly, a main street. It had the look of a small town. All in a row were a hardware store, drugstore, flower shop, boutique. A traffic sign said ROUTE 145. Alice knew the other end of this road well; her high school was on 145. So she had been correct about the diagonal; she was circling the city through its suburbs.

Alice could not take another step. She sat on a bench. It was pretty here, with a row of flagpoles, each pole with a small circle of red, white, and blue flowers. Alice's mother knew flowers and could have named them.

The tears came back when she thought of her mother.

When Alice was little, she had thought of her mother as a goddess: a beautiful, sparkling woman of perfection and strength. It had been so awful, so painful, when her mother turned out to be somebody Alice didn't always like. Okay, other girls moaned and groaned about their mothers, but Alice figured hers would be different; her mother would stay flawless.

No.

Not only did Mom have flaws, but she had left Dad, and for Alice this was a gap in Mom's character that Alice could not forget.

Alice busied herself sorting out the contents of her backpack, tossing the dead snack into a trash container, and taking the price tag off the nerd glasses.

Way down the block, from behind a brick building in whose front yard a fruit tree blossomed, came a police car.

Alice put the glasses on. The corrective lenses made objects shimmer and curve, like heat spots on the road. The police car drove toward her; she could feel the cop's presence, his uniform, his loud voice, his gun, his handcuffs —

But it drove by.

Through the distorting lenses, Alice could not tell whether the officer was a man or a woman. It was simply a person not looking left or right.

Alice had to wait until her heart had stopped jumping around before she could move, and then she had to move, because sitting still was too scary.

Definitely a case, thought Alice, of Why did the chicken cross the road? To get to the other side. I'm that chicken. Short on reasons to do anything.

Gathered outside a secondhand boutique with plaid shirts, prom gowns, beaded bags, and camo pants all in the same window, was a group of girls older than Alice. She thought they were about eighteen. They were loud and very full of themselves. Alice drifted near, keeping their bodies between herself and the traffic on 145.

"So do you like your new roommate any better?" said one girl.

"I hate her guts; she's a jerk," said a girl wearing a State University sweatshirt.

"What are you going to do about it?"

"I dunno. What am I supposed to do about it? I told the dorm supervisor and she shrugs, she says 'Sometimes people have to try harder.'" The speaker was disgusted with the concept of trying harder.

Down the street, driving slowly, came a car Alice knew. Oh, yes! she thought, overjoyed. Mom stayed by the phone, weeping, praying I'd call again, and she sent Richard Rellen out to find me.

For that dark green Volvo wagon, square, solid, and practical, belonged to the man her mother planned to marry.

Alice was trembling with relief. Mom cared. Of course Mom cared; how could Alice have thought for a moment that she did not care? Of course Mom had stayed by the phone, and would be sobbing even harder now, aching and yearning for Alice to call, so Mom could take back what she had said, could explain and apologize.

Alice lifted her arm to wave. She opened her mouth to call, thinking *friend*, thinking *ally*, and thought: Wait. *Over*joyed.

Was she feeling too much joy?

Alice stepped back, trying to be a college girl among college girls.

Her parents had argued over Rick darling. Dad and Mom had said terrible things to each other about Mom's dating. Alice had fled the room and let them have their arguments without her. She hated raised voices, but especially her own mother and father at war.

Through the glimmery focus of her new glasses, she saw Rick Rellen glance at the group of girls. Alice's hair was up beneath her baseball cap, and Alice never put her hair up, because she believed her left ear stuck out, and it was unbearable to let the world see her ear. Now, in nerd glasses, pathetic T-shirt, cap, and protruding ear, Alice wondered if Mr. Rellen would recognize her.

In Dad's honor, Alice had avoided him as much as possible.

She did not know whether she actually disliked Mr. Rellen, or if she was working on it for Dad's sake, or if this was her personal contribution to strife: her way to make her mother pay.

Whatever he was, he was not a parent. Alice was ready to talk to her mother. She was not ready to talk to the future second husband of that mother.

It startled Alice to be so sure of that. It was the first thing all this long hard day that she was sure of: She was not going to confide in Rick Rellen.

"Oh, I know the woman you mean," chimed in a third girl. "She used to be in charge at Flemming Dorm. You're right, Bethany, she never does anything to help you. She says you have to learn to take things in stride."

The girls made noises of disgust and headed for a big, heavy-duty, take-the-class-with-you-to-Disney-World Econoline van. Swivel seats, privacy glass, the works. The girls piled in. Bethany was the driver.

Alice took off her glasses, hoping she looked eighteen and not twelve. "Hey, listen, I hate to bother you," she said, "but can you give me a lift back to the campus? I think my boyfriend has abandoned me here."

It was a sisterhood moment. They had things to do, and they did not want to be bothered, but still, they could not drive away from a woman whose boyfriend had proved unreliable. "Well, okay," said Bethany sullenly.

Alice climbed in, said "Thank you," and sat in back, where she would not bother them. The shock of being pursued had left every joint weak, every muscle trembling. The backseat would be a very short vacation from running.

The State University campus was also on 145, maybe ten miles from Mom's, maybe half that from Dad's or Westtown Mall. So Alice had covered a lot of territory in order to get nowhere.

Ten miles took enough time, however, to ask herself what she was doing, and why.

The van moved slowly out into the traffic.

The Volvo idled beside parallel-parked cars. Rick Rellen's left elbow stuck out the driver's window. Cradled in his hand was a car phone.

Chapter 5

Strangely isolated in the back of somebody else's van and the back of somebody else's conversation, Alice found herself able to reach the back of her own mind. The desire to talk to her mother had disappeared. The need to weep for her father had left her chest.

She began to reconstruct the day.

She'd been home by herself. Dad called. He urgently requested her to leave the house with the disk TWIN and to meet him out of town. He gave her the extraordinary order to drive his most precious possession — a car she could not drive. So Dad *desperately* wanted those disks. Did he just want them — or did he want them out of the house? Had he known that somebody else was about to break in for those same disks? If so, he would have wanted Alice out of the house.

So he did not think Alice was in danger. And he must not have thought *he* was in danger, or he would have barricaded a door, or called the police himself.

Fifteen or twenty minutes had passed before the man entered Dad's condo. So that man could not have been very far away. In a city, however, depending on traffic, ten minutes could mean half a mile or several miles. Everybody Alice knew lived within that sphere. This did not narrow it down.

That man had spoken in a voice Alice half knew. He knew things about Dad, as if they had worked together. He had entered with a key. Presumably Dad's key.

Alice had hid from this trespasser under the Corvette. Time had passed, in which there were strange and awful noises she could not identify, and one she could: the computer keyboard. Then the man left, driving away in that navy blue minivan.

Could the person to whom the voice spoke have been Dad himself? Could Dad have *walked* into the condo? No. He would have yelled; fought; warned his daughter somehow. Had he been carried in? Had that heavy sound, that couch-falling sound, been her father's body when it was dropped to the floor for the police to find? Could he have been carried in unconscious? Had the actual murder of Alice's father taken place while she lay silently sobbing under the car? Could his body have been in that condo while she was showering and changing clothes?

He was a big man. Tall and lean and strong. He was fit. It would take another big strong man to move him. And as for killing him, how could somebody as small as Alice have accomplished that?

But she did not know how he had been killed. If he had been shot, it definitely had not happened at the condo; she would have heard something. Her father possessed no guns; she, Alice, would not have had access to a gun, and her mother would know that. How else do you kill a man? Hit him over the head? Alice wasn't tall enough. Her mother would know that, too!

But there again, the excess of cop shows Alice had seen filled her with an excess of images: You could catch a person by surprise. You could come up behind them. You could get them to stoop down to pick something up and brain them with a baseball bat. You did not have to be bigger than your enemy. Just smarter, or luckier.

But nobody was smarter than Dad!

Alice wrenched her mind away from pictures of herself, from the very pictures her mother must be forming, of the shape of Dad's death and Dad's killer. She forced herself to go on analyzing the events.

She had not entered his bedroom. She had not gone near his bathroom.

Alice had taken the time to shower and change and had driven away in the Corvette, as her father had told her to do.

At least an hour later, maybe an hour and a half, because Alice had no idea how long she had sat, comatose from anxiety, waiting for Dad to arrive, had come the excited claims on the radio that Marc Robie had been murdered; that Alice had sent an E-mail confession to her own mother; that Mom herself called the police; that police were looking for Alice.

Swiftly; everything had happened so swiftly. As if it had been engineered.

Next, Alice had called her mother, who,

in shock and grief and horror, definitely did believe that Alice had killed Dad.

So while Alice lay flat and shuddering beneath the car, something other than murder had taken place. The murderer sent a false E-mail message to Alice's mother. How could the murderer have known the password? How could the murderer have known that Alice signed off Ally when talking to her mother? What possible wording, what possible sentence, could make a person's own mother say — Yes; my daughter killed her father?

Alice could hardly bear to think of her mother. The betrayal! How dare Mom believe so readily!

And if all, or some, of this were true — what vicious and terrible person had trapped Alice beneath the Corvette? A person who would not only kill Dad, *but think of a way to hold Alice responsible*.

The voice had commented out loud on Alice's clothing thrown on the floor. He'd been looking for Alice when he opened the garage door. *What if Alice had not been perfectly hidden?* What if the murderer had seen her on the garage floor? What if he had known all along that Alice was in the condo — and arranged to have the police come, and find her, filthy and sobbing and hiding under her father's car? Having just sent a confession of murder to her own mother?

The back of the van smelled of old food: faint whiffs of abandoned potato chip bags and french fry containers. Alice was so queasy she had to hold onto her mouth and stomach. She ordered herself not to get sick. She had done that once; she was not doing it again. Dad and I were going to eat out tonight at that new Japanese restaurant, the one where you sit in a circle and watch the chef.

She thought: Dad is never going to do anything with me again.

She thought: I know where he was. He was at that number. The number displayed on Caller ID. Either he was killed there, or he was caught there.

She closed her eyes, trying to remember the number, trying to find it in her dark and angry mind. It had been a local call, so the first three digits were 399. The next four ... they'd been a pair ... some sort of match. If only Dad had the newer type of Caller ID, where it also displayed the name!

She remembered the last four digits. 8789.

The van slowed for a speed bump. "Uh — so — um — where do you want to get out?" called Bethany.

Alice was shocked. She had forgotten the van and the girls and the college. She looked out the window, as afraid as she had been when she first heard the voice in the condo.

I can't get out; the van is so safe, dark, and cool.

The van had come to a complete stop.

"This is great," said Alice, stepping forward in a crouch and yanking the door handle down. "You're a peach," she said.

Bethany gave her the tight, irritated smile of somebody who is not a peach and does not want to be put in this position again.

Alice hoped these girls never watched the evening news, didn't care about local crime, but got into fights with their roommates tonight. She slammed the heavy door shut and walked away without looking back. Very difficult. She had not managed it with the Ford, but she disciplined herself, and managed it with Bethany.

What were they saying about her? What observations had they made? What would they do next?

They'll forget me, she told herself. She shivered slightly.

Pathways crisscrossed the grass. Whatever angle you needed to go, there was cement to follow. There was not a bush, not a flower, not a tree to relieve the cement slapped down in the grass. Alice's shadow was like a silhouette on a wanted poster.

It was hard to accept that she must hoist her body and voice and keep going. Keep going where?

The campus was its own city. Each building looked exactly like every other building. Plain brick rectangles, as if the college had not used an architect, but bought buildings off a rack. We'll have twenty dorms, please, ten classrooms, and a lab.

Lab, thought Alice. This campus will have a computer lab. It will be open twenty-four hours, because computer users need to be in there any hour of the day or night.

Each utilitarian building, like the elementary school, was named for a person.

The Joe P. Johanneson Building. The Eunice I. McGarry Center. No clue as to the purpose of these buildings.

Shadows leaped in her face. Shadows rushed past her, and got in front of her, and suddenly Alice realized that the afternoon was late; in fact, it was nearly evening. She was going to need dinner and a bed.

Cars were entering and leaving the student parking lots. Doors were slamming, engines were refusing to turn over, gears were jammed, horns were honked, radios were blaring.

Food she could get. She had a little cash and there would be a cafeteria. But a bed?

How casual the girls in the van had been. How easily they accepted her as a classmate in need of a ride. Could she convince somebody she was just another classmate in need of a mattress?

She walked on, hardly able to tell where she had been, never mind where she was going. The similarity of each building to the next and to the last made each step seem pointless. She was on a treadmill, like one of those pathetic muscular people you saw in gymnasium ads: running, running, running, their little headphones chatting to them, their sweaty backs going no place.

In front of her materialized the Stefan R. Saultman Computer Center. They probably didn't name a building after you unless you had a middle initial. Stefan R. Saultman had more character than the other buildings, and the doors were not ground level. She had to ascend a dozen cement steps to a pair of glass doors so heavy that at first she thought they were locked. Only when she hauled with all her strength did one open for her. She could hardly keep the door open long enough to get through it.

Inside was an attractive room with marble floors, like a state senate. How surprising to see this attention to appearance. Velvet cords hanging from low chrome posts made a little corridor within the room. These led to a second set of doors . . . with an electronic scanner.

INSERT COLLEGE ID WITH PHOTO FACEUP.

The second set of doors smiled at Alice, knowing that she had no ID.

No people appeared, as if she had entered some human-free zone.

Alice stood in the marble silence, immobilized by this defeat.

She nearly seized the velvet rope for a weapon when a living person did come in behind her. She tried to think of an excuse for being so frightened, but the guy who walked in had not even seen her. Even nerdier than Alice was, not just loser glasses and brand X cap and ears sticking out, he also sported pocket protector, Bic pens, and laptop. Alice was pretty sure the whole world was invisible to this guy. She prayed for him to drop his ID card, but of course he didn't, and he passed on through and the inner door shut heavily behind him.

I could have leaped through when he did, she thought. There was time. Should I cram myself through with the next person?

But what excuse would she give for such behavior?

It was interesting that she was still worried about good and bad manners. We murderers must not concern ourselves with appearances, she said to herself, but the joke did not work, because she thought of Dad, and her silly words sewed her lips together, like a dragonfly stitching her soul. She did not believe in the dragonfly myth any more than she believed herself a murderer, and yet —

Her mother believed.

Up the outside stairs came a bunch of boys, jostling and punching and swearing and laughing in the loud way she associated with boys in junior high. She had figured by college you would outgrow this. Alice reminded herself that the worst that could happen was the boys would say No, and she said, "Oh, you know what? I've forgotten my ID. Can I just slip through the door with you?"

They barely glanced at her. Perhaps, like Alice, they had learned to study a member of the opposite sex in one casual, split-second flicker.

They had to line up in order to run their ID cards through the scanner, and lining up did not come easily to this kind of boy. The second-to-last boy in line put his arm out, sweepingly, like an usher about to seat a guest at a wedding, and Alice, hoping she had not misunderstood, let herself be gathered into the line, and she and the boy lockstepped through.

He smiled at her. "I forget mine all the time," he said. "I've spent half the year standing outside the dorm at night waiting for somebody to let me in."

She was blinded by his smile, or perhaps by the relief of being helped. How did people stay on the run? She had been running for only half a day, and already she was so desperate for a hug and some comfort she'd surrender if a policeman appeared right now.

She reminded herself that the police, like her mother, would be a poor source of comfort.

"Come on, Paul, move it," said the last guy, and he, too, smiled at Alice, rather sweetly, as if they had shared something once, and the boys moved it, going down the hall in a group kind of way, bumping and talking in the code of good friends.

She had misjudged them, because of their racket and their pushing. And who, right now, was misjudging Alice?

"Thank you," Alice called after them, but she didn't think Paul had heard her.

Paul.

She was in high school with a computer wizard named Paul. No nerd, that Paul was gorgeous and athletic and a senior and everybody had crushes on him. He had been accepted at awesome institutes of technology — Massachusetts; California — and was trying to decide which one to honor with his presence.

She tried to imagine calling upon that Paul for computer assistance. Or any other kind of assistance. It was beyond possibility. He would not have spent a millisecond noticing Alice, the sophomore.

Of course, he was probably thinking of her now. The whole high school was probably thinking of her now. *Alice?* they were saying to each other. *Sweet dull Alice?*

Not the kind of girl you expect to be a killer, they were probably saying to the television reporters.

It seemed impossible to Alice that she could be a figure on the evening news: the kind they loved to linger on, a shocker. A bloody, cruel, awful shocker . . . and it was Alice.

Oh, like wow, her classmates were saying to each other, *my locker is next to hers. Wonder if she's had a submachine gun in there all this time.*

She tried to imagine herself going back

to that high school, or any high school, under such a cloud.

Cloud?

Suspicion of killing your own father was not a cloud.

It was a forty-foot brick wall with rolls of slice wire on top.

It was prison.

The boys disappeared down the corridor and Alice followed. She hoped they were headed for an open lab, rows of cubicles each with keyboard and screen. When the boys clattered up to the second floor, so did Alice.

She had chills. The place was overly air-conditioned. At the top of the stairs was a lounge, walls lined with vending machines, drinking fountains, padded black vinyl benches . . . and phones.

Was Mommy by the phone? Was she holding the phone book with its quilted cover? Playing with the china cat which held pencils? Sitting on the slipper chair with its pattern of white geese, and its pillow of stuffed sheep? Was Mommy praying Alice would call again?

What about Grandma and Grandpa, in

Florida in their retirement home? Did they know yet?

Her grandparents adored Alice. Alice adored them.

Alice could possibly get to Florida on her credit card.

But — hide out in Grandma's spare bedroom? Abandon her life? Leave her friends and classes? Her wardrobe and her cat?

She wanted desperately to hear her mother's voice. To hear Mommy say, No, no, darling, it was all a terrible mistake, Daddy is fine, he's been out looking for you, and —

She seized the nearest phone, like a trapeze artist seizing the approaching swing. She called her mother.

A strange voice answered. A voice she had absolutely never heard before. A slightly harsh and loud woman's voice. "Robie residence," it said. Alice froze, trying to imagine who it could be, where her mother was.

After the tiny pause, the woman said in a slow, careful voice, "Alice? Your mother is lying down, Alice."

The woman left little spaces between each

sentence to encourage Alice to speak. "I'll go ask her to come to the phone, Alice."

"Who is this?" said Alice.

"This is Detective Burke, Alice."

This is how criminals get caught, thought Alice. They call their mothers.

"Your mother is desperately worried about you, Alice."

Alice hung up, as gently as if she were replacing crystal on a shelf.

Police were between Alice and her mother. Alice could not picture them among the plump quilted pillows, the baskets full of potpourri, and the rows of wooden kitty cats along the windowsills.

Alice leaned against the wall phone, bursting with anger and grief. Police! Invading both Alice's homes, answering Alice's phone, reading Alice's E-mail, possibly — no, definitely — squirreling through Alice's bedroom and possessions and privacy.

She had to call someone. She had to talk.

She thought of Kelsey, of Laura and Cindy and Mardee and Emma. What if one of their mothers answered the phone? *Hi, Mrs. Schmidt, it's Alice Robie; can I speak to Laura please?* And it would be, *Alice, aren't the police looking for you? We don't let Laura be friends with girls suspected of murder.*

Running away meant you left your friends someplace else.

I shouldn't have run, she thought.

But running had come so naturally. And having started, she was not willing to stop.

She thought of perfect Paul in high school, but he didn't know her and she didn't know how to spell his last name. He had one of those very complex names nobody could spell, so nobody used it. They didn't call him Paul Chmielewskiwicz or whatever it was; they called him Paul Chem. She wasn't going to find his number in a phone book that way.

Alice knew who to call. The number on her father's Caller ID display. The number where —

Where he was murdered? thought Alice.

She believed it now, and yet she could not believe it at all. Would she have to see her dead father to believe it? She never wanted to see him anything except laughing and glad to have her around. If they offered her a chance to see him dead, she would refuse.

But how else would she know if it was true?

The telephones were entirely exposed, nothing but a few inches of Plexiglas separating one from another. Alice hoped that the people using the other phones were too pleased with the sound of their own voices to listen in on Alice.

It was time to find out where her father had been. She needed to know who answered the phone at 399-8789.

She rang up the zillion digits required for a credit card call. Her hands hurt just tapping the buttons. Sometimes Grandma could not do crossword puzzles because arthritis made holding the pencil difficult and now Alice knew how it felt; it felt cold and cruel and helpless. You didn't have to be seventy. You could be fifteen and alone.

The phone rang once. A quick masculine voice said, "Yes?"

One syllable. One single ordinary syllable that everybody in America used every day, and Alice had to identify the speaker from that.

I can't, she thought. I don't know who this is, and I don't know if it's one of the voices in the condo. Am I speaking to my father's killer? *Who is on the phone with me?*

She said, "This is Alice."

There was a gasp.

Alice stood very still.

The person on the other end hung up.

Alice's hand did not let go of the phone, but remained curled around the receiver. She did not know who this man was, *but he knew who she was.*

Under the circumstances, it seemed to Alice that any grown-up would have questions for her. Any grown-up would try to keep her on the phone, try to locate her, try to get answers, and bring her in.

Any grown-up except the man who already had the answers.

She got her hand loose. She gave it a piece of book bag to clutch instead and she turned herself around and walked away from the phones. A sign poking off the top of a chrome stand said:

LAB OPEN 24 HOURS
ALL STUDENTS MUST PRESENT ID

But there was nobody checking IDs and she simply walked in and nobody looked up, because people using computers never look up, and Alice circled the room, found a carrel, sat down, flicked on the computer, and there they were, friendly little icons willing to work for her whether she was accused of murder or not.

She took out her father's disk, and she saw his hands, his long thick fingers, strong and clever fingers, taking this disk, entering information on it, possibly dying for it.

She let herself slide into a daydream in which Daddy had met her for ice cream after all, and he said to her, "I'm so proud! You drove all this way without any problems? In the toughest car on earth to drive? Not a scratch on it? Wonderland, you've saved my life."

But I didn't save his life, she thought, falling out of the dream.

He's not going to kiss me eleven times on the hair, and he's not going to play caveman and yank my hair and pretend to drag me over for ice cream.

Daddy called her Wonderland because he said Alice had made his life a Wonderland, and he was the luckiest guy on earth; must have been magic and Cheshire cats that gave him such a perfect daughter.

She was pretty sure that your college ID number was your social security number, and if you didn't type that in, you couldn't boot up. Even if she knew her social security number by heart, which she didn't, she wasn't enrolled here and her number wouldn't accomplish anything. She scanned the busy room, waiting for somebody to get up and forget to shut down the computer.

The room was divided among PCs, Macs, and a dedicated row for Internet use only.

The Internet.

She thought: I know the passwords. I can read my mother's E-mail. I can read what I supposedly sent: the message in which I supposedly confessed to killing my own father.

Chapter 6

Mom i don't know what happened. We got into an argument and we yelled and you know how much i hate yelling and he was asying bad things about you and you know i cant stand when you 2 say bad things sabout ech other and i kept saying stop sotp stop and he didn't and the fight went on and i hit him. mom its awful it really happenede i hit him and i hit him again and i know i have to call 911 but i hid uhndr the car ihstead but i couldn't get away from the blood mommy come get me please come get me ally

Of course she believed it, thought Alice. *I* believe it. It's perfect. Who wrote that? I don't use capital letters when I write E-mail, I don't start with Dear and I don't end with Love, and I say Mom, except when I'm really upset or angry and then I say Mommy. She's the only person who ever called me Ally. I'm an Alice, sort of prim and careful.

Well, she knew now how her father died. He'd been hit. Over and over. There was a lot of blood.

Alice shuddered, and when she fought off the tears, she was not sure whether they'd have been for Daddy or herself. Or even her mother.

How did they think little Alice had done this to her very big father?

There must have been a frenzy in it, a rage, and they must have assumed her father wasn't ready, or had his back turned, or didn't take it seriously.

And they would be right. Only frenzy would make the killer say, "I killed him good," so that Alice could hear. And Dad had *not* taken it seriously, or wasn't ready, or had his back turned.

Suppose Mom read that the moment it came in. This was likely, because Alice and Mom usually E-mailed if they weren't going to see each other that night, and Alice was staying at Dad's. Once she read that, of course she'd have called the police! "Go rescue my daughter! Get there fast! And save Marc."

Mom would have wanted sirens and speed. Mom would have said to herself, it can't be that bad! It can't be!

Mom would have left work, too, rushing, taking *left* turns on red, never mind right, using her horn like a private siren — the way Dad would have loved to drive but Mom would have never dreamed of driving.

The police had been on the way while Alice was bolting in the Corvette; they must have been racing in the front door just as she was racing through the city.

No.

They didn't race in.

Because Alice had thrown the dead-bolt from the inside and closed the garage door. Mom didn't have keys. Who had let them in? Or had they broken down the door?

Dad would have loved that. He had always wanted drama and quick crazy action. Police to the rescue, smashing in the door!

The girl next to Alice was staring at her. Alice was panting: tiny quick little huffs to match an unbelievably quick pulse and an unbelievably bad headache, throbbing and grating with shock.

Alice tried to sit very still. If she could quiet down the leaping ions and screaming synapses of her brain, maybe she could think again.

This terrible confession could probably be used in court. It was so real. Assuming the killer was bright enough to use gloves — and he seemed more than intelligent enough — there would be no fingerprints on that computer but hers and Dad's.

How could Alice combat that confession?

How could she convince people that No, somebody else wrote that?

And there would be other stuff . . . she had scrambled under the car. That rough cement would have scraped off hair, and her terrified fingers pressing down might have found the only grease spots and left perfect prints there, too. And her clothing — the dress that had scraped against the underside of the Corvette was wadded up in the bathroom.

Alice closed the screen, throwing the mouse arrow around until she was out of there, slamming little electronic doors against this nightmare.

Alice stood up stiffly, as a whole group of exhausted, pale girls agreed that this was enough already and gathered their books and notebooks and trudged out of the lab. Sure enough, two had neglected to turn off their terminals.

Alice took a seat, tilted her seat back and looked down the row of college kids.

A gum chewer: jaw barely moving, but moving steadily, unbreaking.

A waist rotater: a girl hoping to find the right word by swaying.

A hair patter: a guy hoping the solution would come if his hair were neater.

A hummer of tiresome tunes, who was about to get socked by the hair patter.

And Alice. Wanted for murder.

She could think of no actual solution for anything whatsoever, but she did have Dad's disk, she could read it. She clung to the belief that on that disk would be what she needed: knowledge, a way out, safety.

She popped the disk into the slot. Moved the mouse. Double clicked.

There was only one file.

She opened it. The fingernails made her crazy. They stuck out far enough so that she hit the wrong keys, or two at a time.

Alice had been expecting scientific material from some company that Dad was involved with at Austin & Scote. Codes and data. Dollars and bank account numbers. Details of some scam or fraud. Maybe even plans to assassinate somebody.

But what she found was her father's autobiography. He was writing about his childhood, and he had started with his own birth. She read several paragraphs. He wrote about the brother Alice had never met, because Uncle Rob died long before Alice was born.

Alice's nerves doubled up on her. She could barely read. The kids in her row were nothing: She was probably waist rotating, hair patting, and humming all at once. But she couldn't tell. That was the definition of losing your mind: when you couldn't tell anymore.

Alice's father wrote: We were not twins. We just thought of ourselves that way. My brother Robert Robie was one year and one month older than I was. Kid, he called me. Or Little Guy. Actually I was taller and heavier. I loved fighting. I was born with fists. I got into wrestling, but my real love was boxing. It was the ultimate challenge: one other guy, one other set of fists. After they found out about it, our parents wouldn't let me box; they were afraid of brain damage. They did let me take self-defense stuff, various Asian disciplines, and those were okay, but I never fell in love the way I did with boxing.

Rob never cared about his body the way I cared about mine.

Like with cars.

I loved cars. I loved high-powered cars, and how acceleration felt against your spine, and how it felt under your foot. I loved the smell of new cars, and the feel of them, and the look of them. I could spend half of every weekend in car dealerships, just looking and touching. I wasn't old enough to drive.

Rob was old enough to drive, and he didn't even care. How could this guy I called Twin be so different from me he didn't care about cars? I couldn't stand an engine that didn't sound perfect, and I believed in a constant program of preventive maintenance. Rob figured if the car started, and he arrived without a tow, that was plenty.

I could never stand a crummy car. Or a crummy body.

But Rob ate enough to keep going, and exercised enough to cross a street, and then he was done.

Alice's mind jumped in and out. Who cared about this? This was more than twenty years ago!

Daddy, you have to help me! she cried. I obeyed you! I took the Corvette and the disks and I went to meet you. You can't let me down. Daddy, I need you now, not twenty years ago talking about your twin who wasn't even a twin!

Alice scrolled quickly, stopping now and then to read a paragraph.

I had short hair because of wrestling; you didn't want to give a guy a grip he could break your neck with, but short hair was not "in" when we were in high school. I had to develop muscles to offset short hair. Believe me, I did. You wanted a great body? Got it. You wanted a great car? Got it. From the time I was born, I knew I had to have a great car and I did yardwork and I washed windows and dishes — about all

a kid under sixteen could do — and I
never spent a cent. You never found me
buying a candy bar or a record. (Cassettes
were just coming in. I didn't buy any be-
cause I wasn't willing to spend my money
on a cassette player.)

She was hungry and tired and deeply afraid and this was a waste!

The disks had nothing to do with it.

Her father had let her down. He hadn't meant to. He had not known that her life would depend on this disk, that she had no other place to go than inside his disk. But there was nothing here.

She dragged the arrow to the end of the file — skipping dozens and dozens of pages — and looked at the final paragraph. Here Dad was talking about Mom and her flaws, and *that* Alice definitely could not look at. That was what the fake-confession-writer had said — that Alice and Dad were fighting about Mom in the first place!

She could sit here no longer, she could stay calm and collegiate not another minute, she could not stare at a computer screen and think; she had to move on.

She'd moved the pointer to the little box

that would close TWIN. Her long strange fingernail was ready to tap. Then she decided to print the file, to read later, in privacy. Not that she knew where to go, where she'd be alone and safe and could turn on a reading lamp.

It took forever to print. Maybe there were too many people in here doing the same thing, or maybe the computers looked good, but were actually ancient, three or four years old.

The printer clicked and buzzed and rattled. It had a continuous feed, and the roll lapped out as if it would never end, and Alice wanted to run screaming out of the room, because it was futile, it was pointless, she had expected a clue, a place to go, a number to call — and all she got was Dad wishing his brother were still alive.

"What are you printing, a book?" asked somebody irritably.

"It's a very long term paper," said Alice. Really, the human body was remarkable. Who would have thought Alice could still speak, and sound rational?

"How many pages were you required to write?" said another voice.

Alice had no idea what length college papers were supposed to be. "This is an independent study."

The printer stopped, in the complete way of computers, as if it had died. Alice tore the last page free, stuck the enormous printout into her stolen backpack and left.

She bought a candy bar from a vending machine, and that would have to be lunch and dinner. Chocolate made her feel a little better. She tried to think of nothing but its silky taste.

Exiting Stefan R. Saultman was easy. Maybe this was always true: Leaving was easy.

She went back out the inner door — no ID needed, but there was an alarm, so presumably if she were skipping out with a computer it would go off. At least she had not done *that* today. Alice held the chocolate bar in her teeth and shoved the heavy glass with both palms to open it.

A lot of time had passed. It was dark out.

It was night.

Night, and Alice Robie was alone with nowhere to go.

Flight had been possible when the sun was shining. But flight in the dark seemed grotesque and terrifying.

The door closed behind her before she realized what a mistake that was. She could have spent the night in the lab. But she was outside now, among unknown buildings, squat and shadowy. The temperature had dropped and she needed a jacket, and she did not know one more thing about her father's murderer than she had known before.

She tried to walk down the dozen cement steps and could not make herself move. Her toe explored, like a little kid testing the water.

A thought quivered up Alice's spine and into her brain. It was a cold thought, and sharp, like crushed ice.

That phone call to her mother. The next call, to 8789.

Mom didn't have Caller ID. But if 8789 had it, he would know Alice had used a State University phone, because all SU phones had the same first three digits.

Half an hour ago, she had told a murderer where she could be found.

Chapter 7

Fingers crept up her shoulder.

Alice leaped away, flattening herself against the wall.

It was Paul of the ID card.

His fingers wired her fears of the dark. The only knowledge Alice possessed was even darker: Alice had nowhere to go.

Paul was stricken. "I'm really sorry," he said. "I didn't mean to startle you."

She could not pull herself together. She could not even decorate her face with a pretend smile.

"You okay?" he said worriedly. He didn't touch her again. She could see him wanting to soothe her, casting for a method, finding none.

"Hard day," she said raggedly. "I'm sorry I jumped." She looked away from him to keep from spilling her story.

The dark was not complete. Every building had spotlights at the corners and doors, and the diagonal paths threading everywhere glowed like white lines on a map.

"What dorm are you in?" he asked. "I'll walk you there. If you wait for the campus escort bus, it'll be fifteen minutes."

So it was a dangerous campus for other people, too, not just those whose location was known to murderers.

Alice tried to have a strategy. I must be a college student, she thought. Somebody three years older than I really am, who actually does live here, and would have waited for the campus bus. "That's very nice of you," she said, and remembering the girls in the van, she added, "I live in Flemming, Paul."

It was his turn to be startled. "How do you know my name?"

"Your friends were teasing you when you let me in. Besides, Paul is a nice-person name." She smiled at him, but it was a failed smile. Her lips didn't cooperate. She tried to breathe again. What would happen when they got to Flemming? What was she to do all these long hours of night? And the next day, and the next?

"So, in what way was the day hard?" said Paul, heading down the last steps.

She went with him. She tried to think of a good lie.

Couldn't.

Shrugged instead.

Paul grinned at her. "Guys with nice-person names try to be sympathetic."

Alice could not help returning this smile. If criminals didn't get caught phoning their mothers, they probably gave themselves up to the first warm smile. "My roommate and I had a terrible fight," she told him. "I can't imagine where I'm going to sleep tonight. I just can't go back to the room." Nice of Bethany to provide her with behavior excuses as well as a dorm name.

Paul nodded. "I'm in a triple. My two roommates and I fight like that all the time. There's never a night when I want to go back to the room."

Since Alice had no idea where Flemming was, she had to let Paul lead, but he was walking at her pace, so the let-Paul-lead theory was not working. They were coming to an intersection of paths and she would not know where to go. "I feel like sleeping on the grass," she admitted.

By day, "grass" sounded green and soft, a place where you might sit and picnic. But at night, "grass" sounded black and cold, creatures slithering over you and nothing to protect you.

Paul took Alice seriously, as if he *had* slept on the grass once. "No," he said, shaking his head. "The temperature's really dropped. It'll get even colder during the night. We might have a frost. Listen, you can spend the night with a friend of mine at Flemming. Her roomie always stays with her boyfriend, so Ginger's got an extra bed. Ginger's on the sixth floor. Where are you?"

Alice felt ruined, hopeless, yet she was able to deduce that sixth might be the top floor, in which case if she said seventh, Paul would know he had a problem here. "Third," she said easily.

"You won't run into your roommate then," he said. He strode to the left and she turned with him, and around the next building was a many-arrowed sign. Flemming's arrow pointed across a major street. Paul hit the Walk button, and they waited patiently for the lights to turn. People gathered around them and she felt strangely less safe in a group.

Alice found herself gripping Paul's arm above the elbow, where the muscle felt as solid as the smile had. She tried to let go, but letting go didn't happen, and Paul did not seem to mind. He said, "What's your name?"

It was Dad who had Other Life fantasies. Dad who liked to talk about changing his name, going underground, becoming a spy. Had Alice, listening to Dad ramble, also planned to become another person with another life? Rehearsed what to say to a future Paul? She must have, because the lie came so easily. "Emily," she told him.

A wonderful fantasy grew in her mind. What if Dad *had* vanished? What a great explanation! That was the answer. Her father was not dead at all, but had run away to begin his Other, more exciting, more dangerous, Life.

How comfortable this idea was. Like a teddy bear. She would cuddle it during the night.

"Emily," repeated Paul. "It's a nice-person name, too." He shifted her with practiced ease, so that she was not gripping his arm, but holding his hand.

Alice had a sudden memory of her first day in kindergarten, when her parents had parked on the far side of the street. To make the big and scary crossing to that vast and frightening school, they stood on each side of her, so she had two hands to hold. She remembered her mother's skirt, her father's khakis.

What could have happened to that happy marriage?

I have to read the printout, she thought. Because I have another mystery to solve. Where did the love go?

She thought: Is Mom afraid *for* me? Or afraid *of* me? Oh, Mom! What can you be thinking about me? We have to talk. But I can't talk to the police. I can't have that horrible E-mail between us.

Paul was telling her about his major. He was studying computer engineering, of course; people who did not understand computers were hopeless. Someday he would have his own company, writing the best software, and people would recognize him on television.

Now that Alice thought about it, she realized that people asked very few questions. Without any hesitation, Paul had accepted her as another college student. What if Paul watched the news tonight and found out otherwise? What if Mom had supplied the police and the network with a photograph of Alice?

It was suddenly gruesome. If Alice were to turn on the six o'clock news, she would see herself.

But it was way past six. The news was over, unless you stayed up to eleven. Alice supposed everybody in college did stay up, but she doubted it was to catch the news.

The Walk light flickered. Paul stepped into the street. Alice did not. She had a sense of ongoing traffic. She half looked to her side and half identified a minivan hesitating before making a right turn on red. There was no mistaking the extreme slant of the front end. Chevy Lumina, thought Alice.

"Come on," said Paul, and she was embarrassed. Her dawdling was annoying this very nice person going so far out of his way for her. She stepped after him and the Lumina accelerated instead of stopping.

Paul knew that traffic was there, but did not bother with it. He had that campus swagger, complete certainty that mere citizens would make way for a college student. He probably rode his bike in the middle of the road and, on Rollerblades, circled in front of traffic to prove he could control them.

Paul reached the curb.

Alice was still in the middle of the road.

The van had manual transmission. It shifted hard from first into second and roared around the corner. The low-scooped front end bore down on her. It was a dark color. Possibly navy. Possibly not. The engine sounded exactly like the minivan that had left her father's. But that van had left her father's slowly and politely, and this van was going to run Alice over.

Alice could not pick her feet up fast enough. It would crush her.

"Sheesh," said a guy behind her. A huge arm gave her both a shove and a lift. Alice and a guy built like a linebacker teetered on the far curb. The minivan shifted into third, way too hard, as if the driver thought he had a Corvette, and then it vanished down the street. Alice heard it go into fourth when she could no longer distinguish its taillights.

If I were going to run somebody over, would I choose a lightweight minivan with crummy power? she thought. No. I'd get a Dodge Ram and obliterate them. Maybe it's a coincidence, two Lumina minivans in one day.

Trembling, Alice touched her rescuer's sleeve. "Thank you," she whispered.

"Hey. No problem. I swear that dude headed right for you."

"I didn't even notice him," said Paul.

"Yeah, man, I saw that." The football guy was laughing. "Didn't you go to kindergarten? Remember? Look left and right before you cross?"

"I was a genius," said Paul. "I skipped kindergarten."

Even Alice managed a laugh.

Paul said to the guy, "Thanks. Thanks a lot."

"Hey. Whatever." Her savior turned left, and Alice and Paul went straight. The inside of her head was clogged.

They arrived at a huge building with several wings. A lot of women lived in Flemming. The front doors were propped open with wooden wedges. So much for electronic ID. Alice and Paul walked right in. Alice tried to act as if she knew every corner.

The ground floor of Flemming was a sprawling, open room with several sitting areas. Girls were slouched on hard-looking purple couches in front of a large television. They didn't look like the kind of people who cared about the news. In fact, they were watching *General Hospital*, which was impossible at this hour. Must be a tape and a VCR, thought Alice, amazed that she was capable of deduction after such a day.

Alice wanted to be at home, at Dad or Mom's, in her own familiar bed with her own familiar pillow, to cry herself to sleep, to make all the noise she wanted while she bawled. But if she gave herself up, she would spend the night in a jail, and she would have company all right, but probably not the kind of company she was used to.

Paul headed for the phones, punched in four digits, and said, "Hi, Ginger."

What if Ginger were the chatty type? What if she wanted details and names and room numbers? If Ginger wanted to talk,

Alice couldn't do it; it would turn out that Alice had seams, like a rag doll, and her seams would burst, and her stuffing would come out.

Paul turned with a smile. "Ginger says it's cool. She's in Six-Fourteen. Go on up."

Complete strangers would literally open doors for her, and give her rides and rooms, and save her when cars didn't look where they were going. Alice managed half a voice. "Thank you, Paul."

He did not seem ready to leave her. He gave her a funny, crooked look and she thought for a minute that he wanted to say something romantic, but she was entirely wrong; couldn't have been more wrong; he wanted to give advice. "Nothing matters that much, Emily. It's only a roommate. You gotta shrug."

She'd forgotten she was Emily. Forgotten she had roommate problems.

Alice dredged up a smile and extended her hand to shake his and he seemed slightly surprised, and maybe amused, but he shook it, and his hand was firm and dry and warm, and Alice wanted to keep hanging on, but she let go and turned and there were the elevators and she walked toward them and her legs worked and everything.

She pressed Up. The elevator door opened immediately. She stepped in. Turned around.

Paul was watching her. He looked uncertain, and she thought, What if he thinks he's done something crazy? What if he says to himself — Is this safe? Is Ginger going to be okay?

So she smiled and waved and hit Six and the doors closed and Paul was gone.

The elevator felt like a cell.

The same space and comfort she would have if the police found her.

The doors opened.

Alice stepped out on Six, and a redhead down the hall was waving cheerfully. "Hi, Emily! I'm Ginger." Ginger was pretty, in a plump settled way, as if Ginger had finished growing up and was ready for marriage and children and a career. Alice felt twelve to Ginger's thirty.

"I haven't seen you around," said Ginger, smiling.

"I'm a freshman," said Alice. "I haven't been very active on the campus."

Ginger nodded sympathetically and

drew Alice into her room. "I have extra sheets if you want fresh ones."

"Thank you," said Alice, "but it's fine, I'll be fine, this is really nice of you."

"I won't tell Barb, and she sure won't notice. I'm off, I have a date, I'll be in late. Just leave the bathroom light on."

"Thank you," said Alice, and she wanted to fling her arms around Ginger and tell her *They all believe I murdered my father,* but she didn't, and Ginger said, "I'll try not to wake you when I get in."

And Alice was alone in somebody else's dormitory.

She stood in Ginger's shower for a long time, hoping hot water would take away pain, but it didn't. She folded her jeans and T-shirt, washed out her underwear in the spray, and scrubbed the peasant dress, yucky from the bed of the truck. She draped the wet clothing on coat hangers to dry in the night. Naked, she slid into the roomie's bed, put her head on the pillow and in spite of her plan to lie there and think things through, and come to a reasoned, logical decision about tomorrow's actions, she was asleep immediately.

When Alice woke up, it was four in the morning. She knew because Ginger had a digital clock whose square numbers gleamed in the dark. Alice could hear breathing, presumably Ginger's.

Alice could not cry because it might wake Ginger up.

She must read the printout. But she was not at home, she couldn't read under the covers; the printout would have to wait till morning.

Wait.

Maybe the disk was *not* the important thing.

Dad had told her to bring the Corvette.

Maybe the car itself was the important thing!

The Corvette. Was there money stashed in some hidden compartment? Some vital paper slid under a floor mat?

Alice's mind raced from thought to thought but refused to complete any real function. She couldn't get anywhere except closer to tears. She wanted to collapse, but she was in a bed; she was already collapsed.

Alice thought she'd been awake all

night, but when the alarm went off in the morning, it tore through her sleep like lawn mower blades.

Ginger had the volume up high. Rock music slammed into every inch of the small room, hard and fierce, bouncing off walls and bookshelves.

Alice hung onto the sides of the bed. She had been in the middle of a dream in which she watched two men kill her father and did nothing to stop them.

"And it's exactly seven A.M. on a beautiful Thursday morning," said the announcer, in a rolling, delighted voice, "and all you people who have postponed getting up since six-thirty, you guys need to throw those cozy covers off, grab the bathroom first, and wake up in the shower."

Ginger obeyed. She threw her covers off. Her comforter and pillow hit the floor and she stumbled to the bathroom and slammed the door, and Alice wanted to turn the radio down, but moochers (and liars) probably did not have the right to adjust volume.

"Police are still searching for the girl whose father was found brutally murdered in his condominium yesterday. Marc Robie, age thirty-nine, was beaten to death. After sending her own mother an E-mail confession, his daughter Alice Robie, fifteen, fled the murder scene in her father's red Corvette. The car was found at Westtown Mall. Several witnesses describe a slender girl with brown eyes and shoulder-length brown hair, wearing a long, flowered peasant dress and white sandals."

That dress was hanging in this room. It was possible, Alice supposed, that Ginger had not seen it. After all, Ginger had come home last night in the dark and, this morning, raced into the bathroom too fast to examine laundry.

Ginger could not have missed a word of that radio announcement. Alice did not hear the water come on in the shower. Ginger was probably barricading herself into the bathroom.

But for some people, radios were just company, and those people did not really ever hear anything. Perhaps Ginger was studying her complexion in the mirror and thinking about her date last night.

I can't hang around to find out, thought Alice.

She, too, flung off the covers, slipped

into her underwear — crunchy the way clothes dried on a line always were — yanked on her jeans and T-shirt, crammed the peasant dress into the backpack, pulled on her sneakers, tied them frantically, slipped out the door, and ran down the hall.

What would Ginger think? If she hadn't known already, she would know now. She would tell Paul. She would say, Thanks a lot, Paul; you put a murderer in the same room with me.

There was somebody standing in front of the elevator, and Alice could not have a conversation, so she took the stairs, flying down six flights.

In a few minutes, when she figured it was safe to emerge from the bathroom, Ginger would call the campus police.

Alice hit the outdoors running, and to her absolute amazement, there were plenty of other runners. People in ugly sweats or impressive stylish running clothes jogged or speed-walked or galloped, all in the same direction, so Alice headed that way, too, passing most people because she had more to run about than they did.

Up ahead was a trail marked with varnished pine signs and a moving feet logo. Here and there were sharp little notices: NO BIKES.

The big backpack flapped against her shoulders and slid down and got in her way and threatened to slam against runners who passed her. "Sorry," she kept saying.

The trail wound through a small woods, down a long, gentle hill, and by the edge of a pretty creek. Weeping willow fronds hung like pale yellow shades.

After six tenths of a mile (Alice knew because the trail was marked every tenth of a mile) the footpath was breached. The runners had to pause, push a Walk light for a busy six-lane road, and cross the traffic to where the footpath began again. The real runners ran in place while they waited. Others stumbled and panted and leaned on the trunk of a tree.

I need a car, thought Alice, watching the commuter traffic. She felt completely capable of stealing a car. She ran her fingers through her long hair in a familiar comforting gesture, pulling it back and then smoothing it down again.

In a red Saturn, Alice's friend Cindy drove by, peering out her car window. Alice stepped behind a jogger whose large gut definitely ought to be slimmed down, but not now when Alice needed it for protection.

Cindy's window was down, and her face was outside of the car, like a dog scenting the breeze. Cindy was the passenger. Her mom was driving, and also craning her neck, as if checking out her side of the street. What could they be looking for? They were miles from the high school, where Cindy needed to be in another ten minutes.

Alice was suddenly aware that the joggers were staring at her, and even the most dedicated had ceased to run in place.

Her ears played back a sentence one of them uttered. "You look like the girl who was on the news last night. The one the police are looking for."

Alice's heart skipped. She made a topknot out of her hair and waved it like a pom-pom. "People have been saying that to me all morning. I can't help it if I have brown hair."

They kept staring at her.

"My gosh, I bet ten people stopped me jogging," Alice said. "Is it my fault I have brown hair? What am I supposed to do — quit my run early? I have two more miles."

The college boy who had accused her actually blushed. "Like wow, I'm sorry. But you know what? I really did just telephone the police." The guy actually had a cell phone on his hip where normal runners had water bottles.

"Oh yikes," said Alice, laughing. "Well, let's hope I have time to take a shower before they interrogate me."

Everybody laughed with her, and everybody crossed the big street together, Alice in the middle, between men's shoulders and women's flapping ponytails.

Cindy and the red Saturn were only half a dozen cars beyond the crosswalk. Cindy's head was poking back and forth.

Alice was pretty close friends with Cindy, who had been through divorce twice with each parent, a horror so enormous that Alice could not even think of it as real life, but as a soap opera taking over. Cindy had been able to nod at everything Alice confided about her own mother and father.

Of course tons of Alice's friends' parents were divorced, and Alice had expected that it would not upset her when her mother began to see other men, but it was hideous.

How could Mom stand the presence of any man but Dad? Couldn't Mom see that these men did not measure up? How could Mom giggle and put on perfume and buy a new wardrobe and experiment with expensive makeup as if she, too, were fifteen and learning how to flirt? And how could she fall for Mr. Rellen, who was old and paunchy and had a prickly beard?

Cindy would say, "Yeah. It's like that, don't worry, it won't bother you after a year or two."

Could Cindy and her Mom be looking for Alice?

I can't waste time thinking about Cindy, Alice told herself. The important thing is that runner. He actually called 911 from his cell phone; from his jogging path. How long before the police show up?

Alice stayed in the pack of runners, or they stayed with her, and in a few paces the trail picked up along the same creek, and there was a sense of country, even though the greenery was just landscaping to screen traffic.

Alice glanced through the leaves and recognized another car. Laura Schmidt's very old Taurus wagon. Laura's older sister was driving. Both Laura and Lucy should be in class this very minute. But no, they were miles away from the high school, cruising a main road. And slowly. Lucy, whose boyfriend had gotten into trouble big time for drag racing at midnight; Lucy, who had gone along and no doubt enjoyed every minute — Lucy was driving half the speed she ought to be, staring all over the place.

The path wound behind a Bagel Deluxe, and Alice slowed her tempo to let the group go on without her. Then she swerved off the trail, crossed an acre of parking lot, and jogged in the back door of Bagel Deluxe. The door to the ladies' room was behind a trellis, which gave a fake, see-through privacy.

Inside, she took inventory. Out of the backpack came the glasses and the baseball cap. Alice threaded her hair through the hole. There was nothing else she could do. She had no makeup, no scissors for a haircut, no pillow with which to gain weight. Alice had read somewhere — or

Dad had told her — that weight gain was the best disguise. Add fifty pounds, and no cheekbone, throat, profile or even hand would look the same.

Along with the peasant dress, sandals, and purse were three copies of TWIN: two on disk, one on paper. This was the kind of stupid decision that gave Dad work: people who subjected all copies to the same risks. She stuck one disk in her jeans pocket.

Get breakfast, she told herself. You have three dollars; get some orange juice, get a bagel. You need calories.

She slung the backpack over both shoulders, tried to pretend she didn't look like the girl described on the radio and shown on television, and left the ladies' room. She would have a raisin cinnamon bagel with cream cheese and then she would feel better.

There was quite a line, but it moved very fast; people knew exactly what they wanted. Alice yearned for food so badly she was embarrassed for herself. She was next. One bagel would not do. She needed two of them, or eight.

The woman two ahead of Alice was juggling a coffee, an orange juice, and a bagel, along with her purse and briefcase and laptop. In spite of this, the woman looked Alice straight in the eye and caught her breath. "Hey — " she said.

"Hi," said Alice, smiling. "I think I recognize you, too. Aren't you Julie's mom? Can I help you carry something?"

It worked. The woman got busy explaining that no, she was Matthew's mom, and Matthew was only six, and probably . . .

"Well, you have a nice day," said Alice, still smiling, and she stepped casually out of line. She walked back out the rear door. She did not have the composure to prevent tears. Tears came in spasms, like a garden hose with a kink. She took paper napkins out of a metal table container to mop her eyes.

Beyond the parked cars was a long, raised, planting area with city-type trees as neat as crayon drawings. Past that was more shopping, with traffic entrances and exits for the next set of stores. It was much too early for any of the stores to be open. In the distance, Alice could see a church spire and the towers of office buildings, glinting like sunglasses. Alice always wondered what held up a building that seemed to be one-hundred percent glass.

Dad worked in a one-hundred percent glass building.

In fact, he worked in one of those.

How far was she from actual downtown? One mile? Two?

The still-rising sun was behind Alice and did not shine in her eyes, but cars turning into the parking lots moved slowly, and Alice thought they could probably not see very well.

And there, most visible, was the car belonging to Paul Chem. As a reward for his brilliance, his grandparents had gotten him a Jeep Wrangler: the real kind, squared off and open, for moving soldiers.

The Jeep was full of guys — three or four of them standing up, hanging onto the frame, looking around and having a wonderful time.

There was no reason for Paul Chem and his friends to be around here; there was nothing here for them; at this hour there was nothing here for anybody; certainly not for high school students who belonged in class.

Only the possibility of finding Alice.

Being hunted by the police was scary,

and yet police did that: They hunted the bad guys. But being hunted by her friends! And these did not qualify as friends — they were just people she would recognize in the hall. Why were they doing it? What sick thrill could they be getting?

Maybe she should not believe her own eyes. She had had several shocks, and not enough sleep or food. Perhaps she was hallucinating. It was an evil mirage: a dancing chorus line of classmates that she was constructing from her imagination.

She found her fingers splayed against her cheeks. She was holding her head up with her hands. Her spine had weakened. Without assistance, she would droop and puddle in the road.

Like Rick Rellen, Paul Chem held a phone in his hand as he drove.

They're calling in to each other, she thought. He's saying, "I checked the K Mart lot and the Twenty Outlets Under One Roof lot. What's my next assignment?"

Was the whole city literally looking for her? Was this an actual team? A squad? People with training? Had somebody said, "Everybody who wants to hunt Alice meet before school, and we'll divide up the city and suburbs and have a hotline so we can update each other."

If this were true, then Alice had become entertainment.

Girl murders father; high school turns out; better than a car wash! Better than a football game!

After all, they're tired of tag sales and bargain hunting. Why not hunt a person? A cheap safari, so to speak. And you get on television if you pull it off.

How dare they!

How dare her classmates turn against her! Hunt her down, eyes scanning crowds, phones ready, gas tanks full!

Alice wanted her mother so badly. Who else could stop this invasion? Who else would know how awful it was, and hug her, and keep her safe?

But to reach her mother . . .

No. There was too much in between.

She could not bear to be caught by these boys. Caught like an animal — a bad dog that had gotten off its leash and had had to be brought home and tied up.

No. They would not catch her.

Alice ducked down behind parked cars

and watched Paul Chem circle. There was no question about his intent. He was searching for something, and it could only be her. Finally the Jeep headed for a distant exit that had its own traffic lights and would leave Paul heading in the wrong direction to locate her.

She stood up, feeling protected by the cars parked behind Bagel Deluxe, but she was wrong.

Paul Chem leaned out of his Jeep, skidded on a turn, and shouted, "Alice!"

Chapter 8

Alice flung herself around Bagel Deluxe and across the six lanes of traffic. Cars would brake in time, or they wouldn't.

Paul Chem would be blocked by the concrete curbs, the raised gardens, parked cars, and a complex series of traffic lights. Would he abandon his precious Jeep and come after her on foot? Alice bet that he would not.

Cars honked as if they were in a marching band. Alice made it across and darted down a side street.

She was on the edge of the city. Low buildings were like foothills before the mountains of downtown. The side streets were all one-way. Alice doubled over a block until she was running the wrong way on a one-way street; the Jeep could not follow her here.

In the distance, a city bus belched smoke as it slowed for a stop. Alice had never been on a bus. Her neighborhood had no public transportation. Was that bus her answer, or was it a fifty-seat trap, and if she got on, strange faces would glint with the thrill of capture, shouting, "You! You're the one!"

She was shocked to hear an engine behind her. This was a one-way street! Cars could only come toward her! She flung a look over her shoulder.

Paul Chem was so eager to capture her that he had taken his precious Jeep and was actually driving against traffic to pursue Alice.

Alice was furious. She fled down an alley. Would this would be like television? Trapped at a dead end by ten-foot-high chain link and topped with rolls of slicing wire?

A garbage truck was backing up as it picked up trash, its automatic horn beeping steadily. Alice squeezed by. The Jeep could not follow. Alice burst out of the alley.

Like pus from a blister, she thought. There was something putrid and stinking about being chased.

Paul's friends would have vaulted out of the Jeep so they could run wherever she ran. Their legs were longer, stronger, and not yet tired. She had no hope.

How would they stop her? A flying tackle? Shove her up against a wall? Grab her wrists and pinion them behind her back?

She raced across another main thoroughfare, fled the wrong way up another street, and through another service alley.

It seemed to her that every face she saw was familiar. She tried to stay sane; she knew she was making this up; these dozens of cars, these hundred faces — they were strangers to her, and she to them.

But one glimpse of a blonde ponytail, and she thought it must be Kelsey.

One glimpse of a crewcut and she thought it must be Michael, who sat next to her in homeroom.

Alice's legs were trembling. She wanted to stop and lean over, brace herself against her own knees. She had fire in her muscles, cramps in her lungs.

What I need, Alice thought, is a car.

She was afraid to look at cars and afraid not to look at them. What if she saw

Kelsey? She wanted to believe that Kelsey had said: Oh no, not me, I'm not going to hunt Alice. I'm going to wait by the phone in case Alice calls and needs me.

I need you, Kelsey, Alice thought.

She had run all the way downtown: towering buildings, international hotels, taxi stands. She walked now and, walking, became invisible; just somebody else headed for work. It was actually still early on Thursday morning. People were still stopping for a cup of coffee, buying a newspaper, getting gas.

The real enemy, Alice said to herself, is not the kids from school. The real enemy is whoever killed Dad. I have to find out who that is. I have to have a plan.

But Alice did not have the faintest idea of what to do next.

She could hardly show up at Austin & Scote asking them to help identify all Lumina owners who had ever known Dad. And if she were to appear at Dad's office, it would be Mr. Austin and Mr. Scote who would pin her to the wall and call the police, instead of Paul Chem.

If she continued through the downtown area, she'd be blocked by the Interstate, which was not the kind of road pedestrians crossed, and by bridges over the river, none of which had walking access.

Alice switched directions. She covered block after block, long blocks one direction, short blocks the other. She was completely without destination. She had only speed.

She felt damaged, as if Paul Chem had run over her. As if she had tire tracks on her heart. She had no friends. Only people who knew her and wanted to bring her down and bring her in.

The fact that this was *her* — plain old nice Alice — got harder to believe, instead of easier. The inside of her mind swayed, like a swing in the wind — nobody sitting there.

To her astonishment, the university appeared again. She kept forgetting how big it was, how much space a place that educates forty thousand people takes up.

On this rim of the campus was a one-story building painted a friendly yellow, with an immense balloon bouquet sign that reminded her of the wooden ice-cream cone at Salmon River. A driveway curled up to the front door, and a wide canopy shaded idling cars.

It was a day-care center.

Each parent left the car running while they went in with a child.

Cars facing out of the city.

Cars full of gas.

Cars ready to go.

Alice could have her pick.

There was an old Dodge sedan, a Voyager with *three* car seats, a cute little sky blue Toyota pickup, an old fake-wood-sided station wagon, and a beautiful black Mazda RX7.

Alice was giddy with choice.

Everybody expected her to be on foot. Nobody would be looking for her in a car. In fact, everybody would have an exact description from Paul Chem: baseball cap, glasses, jeans, and T-shirt, and most of all, the alley where he'd lost her.

But in a car, without cap, without glasses . . .

The mother getting out of the blue Toyota truck unloaded a huge tray which had been resting on the front seat bench. Alice was close enough to see cupcakes, iced in pink with tiny white candles, and the little girl whose birthday it was looked about three. The girl was wildly excited and the mother said, "Don't make me spill," and the little girl held the door for her mother.

It would take time to deliver those cupcakes, discuss the birthday with the teacher, kiss the birthday girl good-bye on such a precious day.

This was the car. A blender if there ever was one. Nothing slid into traffic more easily than toy trucks. In that Toyota, Alice could be miles away before the police got here. Then she could abandon the truck and take another one, before anybody guessed it was Alice who had it.

The mother and the three-year-old disappeared inside the day-care center. Big yellow doors shut behind them. The engine of the little truck burbled in a friendly, picture-book kind of way. Other fathers and mothers drove up, hopped out, and carried, pleaded, argued, scolded, kissed, hugged, and waved.

Not one parent paid any attention to any other parent.

Absolutely nobody was going to notice a thing. This was the moment.

Alice didn't pause for a second.

She walked away.

She had not committed murder, and she could say so, and it would be the truth, whether they believed her or not. But if she took that truck ... if she really and truly drove away in another person's car ...

She could never have faced her parents.

Parents, thought Alice. I have only one parent now.

What must her mother be going through? Surrounded by police and neighbors and acquaintances and business colleagues? All of whom believed that Christina Robie was the mother of a girl who would bludgeon her own father?

I have to let her know I'm all right, thought Alice. Except, I'm not all right.

She wondered if the E-mail message had been displayed or read aloud, on television. What if all Mom's friends, and all Alice's friends, had read and believed?

Alice felt computerized. She had functions and, until her plug was pulled, would go on calculating. But she could not actually think.

Alice dragged herself onto the campus. It was crawling with police cars. They're not looking for me, she said to herself. There's probably a big game; they're here to manage traffic at the stadium.

Right. On a Thursday morning.

Big game, she thought. I guess a girl who killed her father counts as big game. I guess this is now a hunting preserve.

Why must the campus be so barren? Why were there no little copses of trees, little gatherings of flowers, little quadrangles of benches and sculpture?

When she saw a sign for Flemming she knew she was going there. It was familiar, and she was desperate for a safety zone.

"Alice," said a voice right next to her.

This is it, she thought wearily. It's over.

She turned slowly, to see which pursuer had pulled it off.

It was Rick Rellen. He had pulled the Volvo over when he spotted her, not bothering to park, and the bulky square car was angled awkwardly. His graying beard partially hid a smile. He stretched out his arms to hug her. They had never hugged. They had hardly ever even spoken. "Alice, honey, your mother and I are so worried about you! I am so glad I found you!"

Mr. Rellen was a leisurely, hefty sort of man, the type who liked a soft recliner in front of a large TV. Alice's father was tall and thin and never had time for TV. He had too many projects (done with such neatness and care that outsiders thought he had no life).

How reassuring Mr. Rellen's arms looked. How badly Alice wanted to be held and reassured by a parent. Once, Mom had told Alice, Rick darling had gathered her in his arms and carried her over his threshold. Alice had found this more nauseating than romantic, but right now she wouldn't mind being scooped up and carried away from her troubles.

This is the man who is going to marry my mother, Alice told herself. She tried to be as glad to see Mr. Rellen as he was to see her. She tried to tell herself that the two best people to sort this out were her mother and her future stepfather.

Richard Rellen's hand, big and thick, stretched toward her. "Alice, come on home with me." His stout belly was draped with a fine thin sweater, camel colored. The white and gray and black hairs of his mustache and beard gave him a porcupine look. The smile continued. There was so completely nothing to smile about.

"Come on, Ally, let's head on home," he said, getting closer to her.

As if it were his home. As if he could invite her there, like a guest, to her very own house. Even calling her Ally, as if when she was not looking, he had become part of the family. As if Mom and he were married already, and she, Alice, was the outsider.

"It's all a misunderstanding, Ally," he said.

Alice felt as if a painter had put several coats of polyurethane over her thinking. Thinking was down there, beneath the slick layers of shiny stuff, but she couldn't get to it.

"We need to get home," said Mr. Rellen, his smile growing wider. "Talk to your mother, sort it out."

Maybe the Hunter always smiled when he closed in on the Victim.

I'm not a victim, thought Alice.

She leaped away and he leaped toward her, the awful, thick, hairy arm like an anaconda wrapping around her, and in spite of his weight, he was quick.

Alice was quicker.

He didn't get Alice, he got the backpack. He yanked, trying to lasso her with it, but she shrugged it off and raced away. Her flimsy sneakers actually came apart, and just as in nightmares, she knew she was not running fast enough. She circled a huge brick building, half-circled another, left the path, raced across a parking lot filled with hundreds of student commuter cars, and cut between cars parked too close together for Richard Rellen to fit. She sat on the chilly pavement between two cars, invisible to the world.

He had not yelled for help in capturing her. He had not shouted to the students brushing through and around them — This is the girl, don't let her get away! He had allowed her to get away.

Mom must have given him instructions when she sent him out to search for Alice. What could those orders have been? Don't upset her, keep smiling, pretend it's just a misunderstanding, don't use force.

Alice got up, dusting grit from her clothes, and walked along the edges of the commuter parking, mentally noting the cars whose drivers had not bothered to lock. If she got really desperate for shelter, she could slip into a backseat and huddle down.

There was Flemming.

A police car idled by the front door, its radio spitting unintelligible information.

The police would be checking the girls leaving Flemming, not the girls entering. Dripping with sweat, hair hanging in her face, T-shirt wet and jeans clinging, Alice jogged into the dorm.

Indeed, a young officer in a fine blue uniform was asking three college women for their IDs. They were half flirting, and had him completely surrounded, and he did not look up to see who was coming in.

She went to the stairs, not the elevators. She went to Three, for no reason except her legs could climb no higher.

There was little action on the third floor. The few girls who had no morning classes were slopping bleary-eyed between rooms, old saggy bathrobes hanging open, or wearing nothing at all. Flemming Third seemed to be very comfortable with nakedness.

"Oh, like wow!" said a nude girl, laughing at Alice. "You are in desperate need of a shower."

Alice nodded. This had never been more true.

"I've got to take up running," said another girl, coming out of Three Twelve. She was beautifully groomed and had ironed her khaki trousers. Her shirt was crisp, with a pleated front, and a heavy necklace of brown and black beads hung like a scarf. "I haven't done anything since September except lie around." She examined Alice closely. "Do you run every morning?" she asked. "I might join you."

The naked girl giggled. "Please, Amanda, you're never going to take up exercise. You are morally opposed to sweat."

"I would certainly not run fast enough to sweat," agreed Amanda.

Everybody laughed. The naked girl disappeared into Three Fourteen and Amanda followed her. "You owe me a bottle of shampoo, Kerry. I need it."

The hall was now empty. Every door, however, had been left open so that conversations could continue.

"Amanda, you don't need it. You're clean

and perfect. Tomorrow you might need it, but not today."

Alice shivered badly and walked into Amanda's room. Empty. Amanda's roommate must have left already. The bathroom door was open a few inches. Alice slid in. There was no tub and the shower had a glass door. It, like Amanda, was scrubbed and polished. No soap scum here.

Alice got in the shower and closed the glass door, and bit her lips against hysteria. Alice, the girl who hides behind clear glass.

Surely Amanda did not need to come into the bathroom again. Amanda looked like a woman prepared for a sophisticated and successful day, not a woman who still needed to brush her teeth.

Amanda came back into her room. There were straightening sounds, drawer-closing sounds, hanging-it-back-up sounds. Alice tried not to think or breathe. Amanda opened the bathroom door.

Alice pressed her spine against the cold bathroom tiles.

She needed air desperately. Fear used up so much oxygen. Alice needed a bucket of air, a whole room full of air —

Amanda plucked a gold lipstick tube off the counter and left.

Alice's breath came sucking in like the drain in a whirlpool, noisy and unmistakable. But Amanda was already out the door, pulling it shut behind her, and testing to be sure it had locked.

Alice stayed in the shower stall for a long time before she could emerge into the light. Then she searched Amanda's room.

Amanda lived the way she looked. Socks were neatly folded at one side of the top drawer, and the ironing board tucked carefully in the back of the wardrobe. The edges of books had been straightened and a stack of CDs was perfectly aligned. Alice had lived with a person like this.

It hit her once more. Alice *had* lived with a person like this.

Oh, Daddy!

Scissors lay neatly in the top shallow drawer of Amanda's desk. When she was six years old and got tired of cutting Barbie's hair, Alice had given herself a ragged hideous haircut. Should she do it again?

Vanity stopped her. She was going to get caught, or would turn herself in, or solve this, or get killed trying, and she didn't want a disgusting stupid haircut when she had to face the world.

On top of her chest of drawers, Amanda's barrettes and scrunchies were neatly arranged on a silk scarf. Alice took a clip from which tiny shiny ribbons and beads hung, gave herself a spiky topknot, and fastened it with the clip. Never, not once, had she appeared in public with her hair sprouting from the top center of her head.

Then she raided Amanda's wardrobe. "I promise to wash them and starch them and send them back in plastic bags in perfect condition, Amanda," she said to the neatness of the room.

Alice yanked a heavy sweatshirt over her sweaty T-shirt, and on top of that, buttoned up a poufy-sleeved white granny blouse. Then she added a final layer: a long baggy brown and gray dress with ruffles. Alice was always surprised that this style had taken off: ugly white shirts under limp country dresses in which no girl ever looks pretty and she was now fat besides. She hoped Dad was right — weight gain was the best disguise.

She rolled up the legs of the jeans, so

they didn't show below the hem of the long saggy dress. She patted the jeans pocket, which now contained her only remaining possession: the backup disk.

Hoisting some of Amanda's books, Alice held them in her arms in front of her. In the hall, nobody was around. She went back down to the lobby.

Now there were two police officers, a man and a woman, and they were being assaulted by several young women shrieking that cops had no right to invade their privacy! No right to demand IDs! No right to be here at all! Did they want a lawsuit brought against them? Did they understand what worthless revolting excuses for people they were?

Alice joined this promising group, and they all shoved through with much yelling and calling of names and even turned back to glare and shake fists. The police let them go.

Alice was pretty good on essay tests, where the whole key was bluffing. Some teachers never seemed to mind if you didn't include a single fact. They gave you points for length and process. But Alice had not expected life to be like that. Whoever pretends the best wins, she thought.

The book edges dug into Alice's stomach in a familiar, school-type way. She felt sure of herself holding these books, as if the only tests ahead were academic.

She also felt fat. It was most peculiar to have thick arms and such a substantial waist.

Okay, she thought again, there is no point in running unless you have a place to run to. So. Who is at work? Whose house can I hide in?

She really knew that hiding was not going to accomplish a thing. She knew nothing she was doing was sensible. She knew that the only hope of ending this was to end it.

But she kept those thoughts as distant as possible, because she was not ready. She could not deal with her father's death at the same time as answer the questions of authorities. She could not weep for Dad in the presence of a mother who had ceased to love him. And along with all that — perhaps before all that — she could not admit defeat.

She walked, and nobody on the campus

glanced at her — not police, not students, not professors.

Finally she thought of Mr. Heddig, with whom Dad went fishing a few times a year. The men also liked to go to a wilderness lodge for a long weekend. Alice had sometimes gone along. It wasn't like any wilderness she'd ever imagined: The motel room had a Jacuzzi. Alice liked a wilderness that came with a Jacuzzi.

Mr. Heddig traveled a great deal for business. Alice had been to his house the times they went fishing. He's been divorced forever, thought Alice, so there can't be anybody else home. He'll certainly be away during the day, and if he's out of town, I'm all set.

Alice was desperately hungry, but her few dollars and her credit cards were in the backpack in Mr. Rellen's custody.

Alice crossed the huge campus safely and cut through an even larger parking lot than Westtown Mall's, serving a total of nine superstores like Home Depot and Office Max.

People were buying outdoor stuff: barbecues and lawn chairs and flats of flowers and pink flamingos. They did not dress up to do this. Women and men in sweatsuits pushed massive metal shopping carts into which they dumped pet food and building supplies. Dumpy Alice looked just fine.

Alice went to The Brick Oven, where they usually gave away free slices of bread to entice you to buy the whole loaf. Sure enough, they handed her a slab of soft hot bread, and yes, Alice wanted a whole loaf, or ten, but she had no money. She went into Best Price Foods and checked every aisle for food samples and had two crackers with a new cheese spread and one slice of hot dog about the size of a quarter. It was all she could do not to lick the table.

She walked on out, holding her books, as if every schoolgirl routinely stopped in for cheese on Thursday morning.

Was it really still morning?

Was it really only one day since the chase began?

Half a mile past the superstores, as she walked briskly down a sidewalk, alone and exposed, she saw Kelsey. Kelsey, whose parents would rather she had lice than miss a class. Kelsey was cutting school. Kelsey's dad was driving.

Alice hunched down into her books. She tried to look heavy. It worked. She really was a different person. Gone the thin, graceful girl with long, shiny, swinging hair. Alice had vanished. Even her best friend did not know her.

It took her the afternoon to walk to Mr. Heddig's.

He lived on a dead-end road in an old, failed development, where only a dozen houses had ever gone up, had sold poorly and at a loss, and where people did not keep up their yards. Her father could not stand this sort of thing: People should edge their walks and prune their bushes and clean their gutters. It was surprising that he would be close friends with a guy who never thought of that stuff.

The woods had grown thick where people had given up mowing, and hedges planted years before had become green monsters separating each house from its neighbor. Mr. Heddig's house not only looked vacant today, it looked as if it had been vacant for months.

Suppose Mr. Heddig was inside catching up on his sleep after some jet-lag trip to Japan?

Suppose Alice broke in and he kept a gun by the bed and shot her?

Suppose she just knocked on the door and said, Hi, Mr. Heddig, it isn't true, I didn't do it, please let me sleep on a real bed and don't call the police.

Alice knocked on the door.

Chapter 9

Nobody came to the door.

Alice walked around the garage and from a hook hidden beneath a hanging light fixture, she took the spare house key. The weekend of the fishing trip, Mr. Heddig had carefully shown her its location in case she ever needed it.

Inside, his house was dusty and dry, as if it were all attic. It was a split level, and Alice went up the half-stair to the living room/kitchen part. Everything about the house felt tired. Seats sagged and curtains drooped. No wonder Mr. Heddig went fishing a lot. Who would want to stay here?

The only place that looked used was the kitchen counter, littered with the usual calendar, phone, newspaper clippings, Post-Its, business cards, pencils ... and car keys.

In a split level, the garage is beneath the bedrooms. Alice went down the two sets of half-stairs, through a murky rec room, and into the garage.

Yes. There was a vehicle to go with the keys on the kitchen counter. It was a miserable excuse for a car. An ancient Dodge Dart, mustard yellow and rusted, vinyl upholstery baked clear of color and dashboard cracked. A metal dog grate had been fastened between the backseat and the driver's seat, but there was no longer any sign of a dog.

Alice wished there were a dog. She could use a warm, cuddly, tail-wagging body right now.

Alice turned off the garage light and went back upstairs. She was amazed that these dark unknown spaces did not frighten her. Perhaps you reached an upper level for fright, where there wasn't more of it.

She checked the refrigerator. Mr. Heddig definitely ate all his meals out. A stick of butter. Half a jar of spaghetti sauce with mold on it. Ketchup, mustard, pickles, jam, artichokes in a tiny jar, like dead squid.

And a twelve-pack of Coke.

She yanked the pull tab on one can and drank eagerly.

There was food in the freezer, but she could not bring herself to thaw a hamburger patty in the microwave and cook it. There was food on the shelves, but she did not want shredded wheat without milk, and she did not want to heat a can of soup. It was bad enough to be trespassing, but what if Mr. Heddig came home and found her stirring ingredients, setting the table?

Mr. Heddig's kitchen phone was white, the only bright object in the house.

Mom, she thought blurrily.

The phone was in her hand before she could argue with it, but again Alice was not ready to talk with Mom.

If I call Daddy's house, she thought, I'll get his voice on the answering machine. I can still hear Daddy talk. He's dead, but I can still call him up and he'll say who he is, even though he isn't.

Unbearable.

She flipped open the phone book and looked up the billing number. The service person answered so cheerily that Alice knew this woman was small and chipper and had just had her hair done and was looking forward to her favorite TV show that night. "How may I help you?" asked the happy phone person.

Let's see, thought Alice. Money, car, plane ticket, mother, angel ... "I have a billing problem," she said. "There's a long-distance charge to my phone and I don't recognize the number. Would you please look up 399-8789 and tell me who I called?"

"Surely!" said the operator happily.

It's that easy! thought Alice. They'll tell me whose phone it was that Dad called from, and then I'll know who his killer is, and then —

"And what number is it charged to, please?" asked the operator.

Alice's heart sank. The supposedly incorrect bill would be brought up on the computer screen, so the problem could be corrected. But this was also to make sure Alice had a right to the information. There was no bill on which 399-8789 had showed up as a long-distance call. Since Dad's number also began 399, she couldn't give that number to the operator. In spite of how far she had hiked today, Mr. Heddig's phone wasn't long distance to 399, either.

Alice opened Mr. Heddig's address book

and read off a phone number at random.

The cheery voice was puzzled. "I don't recognize those digits," she said. "Are you in the right area code?"

"I'm so sorry," said Alice, and she hung up.

I have no weapons, thought Alice. She called her father's number. After three rings, her father's voice said, "Hi! You've reached Marc Robie and Alice Robie! We can't come to the phone right now, but please leave us a message and we'll get back to you."

No, Daddy, thought Alice. You won't get back.

Alice put a dish towel over her face and bit it, and scrunched the ends of the towel in her fists, and tightened her fingers until the joints hurt. Little creaking sounds came out of her, as if she had rusted from tears and didn't work very well anymore.

She punched in the code to listen to the messages waiting for her father. There was only one. A person who hadn't been listening to his radio, or else lived in another state, said, "James here, Marc. I've been checking the chat room, and there are quite a few responses. Why aren't you logging on? What's happening? How come you haven't gotten in touch? Do you have plans for the weekend? Call me as soon as you're back, Marc."

Plans for the weekend. Dad had planned to take Alice to the movies, and they would have popcorn drenched in butter and large orange sodas, and afterward they would critique the actors and talk about which movie they'd see next time.

That, then, was death. When your plans for the weekend didn't matter. When your plans for your life didn't matter, because you would not be there.

Alice hauled herself up to the bedrooms but could not bring herself to lie directly on a bed. It would be like Goldilocks, and the Three Bears would find her.

In the bathroom was a linen closet. Dad had one set of white sheets, which he took straight out of the dryer and put back on the bed. Mom had sheets with flowers and sheets with lace and sheets in dusty rose, sheets in cotton and flannel. Mr. Heddig just had stuff crammed between shelves.

Alice tugged at the wrinkled mess, getting an ugly peach stripe with yellow and blue dots. It was the kind of reject that traveled from one tag sale to another. But it was clean. She wrapped herself up like a mummy and shuffled down the tiny hall to peek in the bedrooms. She rejected the king-sized bed because it must be Mr. Heddig's.

The second bedroom was used for storage.

The third bedroom had absolutely nothing in it but a bare mattress. "Have a lot of overnight guests, Mr. Heddig?" Alice mumbled. She flopped flat on the mattress, safe in her sheet, sobbed once, and was asleep.

When she woke up, it was dark.

She woke cleanly, without confusion, and without fear. Through the window, stars glittered with unusual clarity: separate tiny speeches from heaven.

Alice scrambled her sheet into its original mess and went into the bathroom. She pulled the shade down so she could turn on the light. Then she stuffed the sheet back onto its shelf. She brushed her teeth with her finger and Mr. Heddig's toothpaste. On the bathroom window was a little plastic sign announcing that the house was wired to prevent robbery.

Alice was glad that she had not seen that when she let herself in. Either the sign was fake or the system was off. At least she could be sure there was no alarm on the miserable old Dart.

Alice felt her way down the three sets of half-stairs and into the garage. Even though she was pretty sure no neighbor could see this house, and pretty sure the neighbors were asleep anyway, she wanted to stay dark and invisible.

This was not the kind of place with an automatic garage door. She hoisted it from the inside. The blackness of night came in, like snakes around her ankles. There was rustling in the trees, and she thought of rabid raccoons staggering over to sink their teeth into her. She tried not to give in to stupid fears (not when she had so many rational fears to call upon), and as she struggled with the heavy garage door, a strong yellow light burst on, like a gunshot without the gun.

Alice screamed, but caught her scream

in time, choking on it, so it was a half-scream.

Mr. Heddig must be home! He had come home while she was asleep. He had heard her prowling around in his house and turned on the spotlight.

Paralyzed in blazing light, Alice was on exhibit for the rabid raccoon or the armed Mr. Heddig. She could not hold the garage door up any longer. Either she had to let go and it would crash down, or she had to shove with all her might, to slide the door into ceiling position. Alice shoved. The door squealed. She was so afraid of the rabid raccoon that she could not bring herself to hide in the bushes, and so afraid of Mr. Heddig and his shotgun she could not bring herself to hide in the garage.

But nothing happened.

No shout. No footsteps. No door opening.

The light, she realized at last, was a motion sensor.

Mr. Heddig was not home. There was no shotgun and no rabid raccoon.

To test her theory, she walked across the front lawn, and sure enough, a spotlight by the door came on. Alice might as well have been playing ball in a night stadium.

Nobody came to the door or yelled.

Alice stopped worrying about the neighbors. If they saw the lights go on, that was all they'd see — the lights going on.

Alice got into the Dart, backed it out, put it in park, climbed out of the car and closed the garage door from the outside. The act of facing the wheel, the act of her feet on pedals, the act of latching her seat belt, calmed her.

Alice drove away.

She drove away in a car that belonged to another person. She could no longer pretend to be a little girl who had made a silly decision. She was a young woman who had knowingly stolen a car.

Alice had never driven in the dark. She was unnerved at how little she could see. She had to guide herself by the single yellow line in the center of the road. There were no side lines, so she couldn't tell where the edge of the road was, and her headlights seemed to point at the wrong thing, as if they or she needed to be lined up differently.

How quickly the car covered ground.

Half a day's walking was minutes in a car.

As she got back into the city, lights were everywhere: every pole, every corner, every building. Alice had the roads to herself. She got lost twice because the glare of the lights and the silence of the streets confused her. She wondered what time it was. The Dart was so stripped down it didn't even have a clock. It didn't even have a radio!

She found her way to Dad's.

She paused by the condo mailboxes, which were on the left side of the entrance, so the driver could pull up next to his box and take the mail without getting out of the car. The spare key was still taped to the inside top of the box where you couldn't see it, could only feel it. She peeled it off. The Scotch tape felt dry and yellow against her thumb.

She pulled into Dad's car-length driveway.

Her headlights illuminated bright yellow tape around the rim of the front door. The tape would not stop her from getting in, but it would certainly be visible that somebody had broken the police seal.

Alice wondered if it would scare her to

be in the condo, where Dad had been dropped to the floor, as if it wouldn't hurt him. Would the ghost of her father linger in his bedroom?

There was nothing she'd like more than some ghost of Daddy.

Alice put the key into the garage door instead, and it opened, softly — *and there was a car there.*

For a moment Alice wanted to scream, but then she realized it was Dad's Blazer. Somebody had brought it home. Alice drove Mr. Heddig's Dodge Dart into the space that belonged to the Corvette, got out, put the garage door back down, and turned the handle to lock it securely. She was home.

Right away she wanted her toothbrush.

She moved quietly through the condo, turning on no lights, feeling her way, wondering if the police had been smart enough to leave a cop here, just in case; wondering if she would touch living flesh when she reached for her toothbrush.

But she didn't, and the bathroom was an interior room without windows, so when she had shut the door, she turned on the light, and the ordinariness of a bathroom she knew was enough to make a person weep, so she wept.

Then she turned off the light and edged over to her father's desk. In utter darkness, she felt the shapes and squares of his computer setup, his files and notebooks. Around her the loneliness expanded and pressed against her skin. Her hands trembled like little puppets.

She couldn't turn on the computer where it sat now. Even with the blinds pulled, the glow would be visible through the living room windows. Condo neighbors knew nothing about each other, but they certainly knew there'd been a murder here. She must give them nothing to notice.

She could unplug the computer, and lug it and the keyboard and screen one by one to her bathroom. Plug them in where your hair dryer or razor went. Shut the door, turn on the light, and work sitting on the bathmat. For a minute this seemed rational, but then she remembered there was no telephone outlet in the bathroom, and she was not going to use the Internet without a phone line.

She went into her room and pulled her

favorite big white blanket off the bed. Rigging it as a tent over her head and the desk, she went to work beneath the folds. The world consisted of Alice and the screen.

Alice booted up. The computer screen gave her the time. Two-thirty-eight A.M.

She put in Dad's password and brought up his address book. She did a search for James, then for Jamie, then for Jim. There were six. Four had E-mail addresses. No last name was familiar.

She wished Dad had kept a list of the cars everybody drove: then she could look up Lumina minivan. Who out there was attracted to the spaceship look? But that was the kind of thing Dad simply knew by heart.

Then she steeled herself. She would write to her mother by E-mail, and this would be the real thing: From Alice: To Mom.

She began to type in her usual careless way, hitting wrong keys.

Mom i did not write that message you got. the person who killed dad wrote it. how could you belive it anyway? you know i adore daddy and i would never hurt him and fort aht matter i would never hurt anybody else either! you did the right thing claling the police because if dad had still been alive he needed an ambulance i didn't even know he was there. whoever it was came in twith a key and i hid under the corvette because i thought he was scary a murderer or something. i was right, but it wasn't of me, it was of dad. he must have killed dad someplace else and brough t his body into the condo and i don't know how he did that, because dad would have been hgeavy and hard to move. but dad had called me just beofre that happened and told me to take a computer disk and drive the corvette to meet him at salem river yhou know where we always went for ice cream and i almost called you for advice because it was such a weird thing for dad to say — drive the corvette when he never let me touch it and i don't even have a license — so i knew it was very important — and i didn't call you because youd say never and i didn't want to let dad down. mom i did not know what had happened int he apartment. the intruder left and drove away and i got out from under the corvette and i left and drove away. i didn't look for a body. it wasn't me, mom. don't have the funeral without me, mom. i have to be there, i know what dad would want, and i'm the one who will miss him i'm the one who loved him. not you. i miss him so much its hard to think. i want him to tell me what to do and he isn't alive to tell any of us anything. then when i found out on the radio about dad anjd about how you believed i had done it and about how you had a confession — well you dont. its something the killer typed and i don't know how he knew but he did.

Alice read what she had written. The message sounded insane. Usually, since E-mail skipped caps, punctuation, spelling and paragraphs, it had a sloppy, friendly look. But this looked demented. It looked like the work of a person whose wiring had crashed.

Far from explaining the situation to her mother — and to everybody who would read it over her shoulder — it would make things worse.

She would have to rewrite, and get her

version in the correct order, and delete the part about the funeral, and —

No. It was impossible. She could not talk to her mother about the death of her father on some dumb computer.

Alice inserted Dad's TWIN disk into the computer's slot and scrolled down to where she'd left off at the college lab.

In a few hours, it would be another day, and this time she could not just trot around, hiding and flinching and fearing and sobbing. She must do something intelligent.

When she finished reading these entries, would she have knowledge, the way rockets have liftoff?

Would she know what to do next?

Chapter 10

I wanted Rob to be just like me. I wanted Rob to pay attention to what I was doing, and imitate me. I told Rob I should have been the big brother, but Rob just grinned and went his own way. Rob was into computers. It was embarrassing then, because home computers were scarce, and only a failure with no friends and no abilities played with computers. It wasn't that people were laughing at computers; your book club and your bank and your gas credit card were computerized. But people didn't use them at home yet.

Rob could do anything with a computer.

Small companies who were using computers floundered around, trying to figure out how to get payroll attached to that computer, how to get inventory stuck inside that machine, how to get it to print,

*how to set it up on the page. Rob worked
with them, and even had fun, the way I
had fun with people who sold cars.*

Alice had a headache. Far away in the
medicine cabinet was aspirin, but Alice
could not gather the energy to struggle to
her feet, fumble her way into the bathroom, hoist a glass, fill it with water, and
swallow. The headache grew until it was
like having another person under the tent
of her blanket.

*So I'm the kid brother, begging for jobs
at car dealerships, promising to clean
trade-ins, be the guy that gets the gum out
from under the driver's seat and squirms
into the trunk to scrub where a quart of
antifreeze fell over two years ago. And Rob
is the big brother, writing programs for
people two or three times his age who are
ready to have computers but don't know
how.*

*And then a guy named Arren hired my
brother Rob.*

Remember, computers are new.

People don't understand them.

* * *

To whom was this file addressed? Alice wondered. Dad was talking to somebody. He had an audience in mind. Was it Alice?

She didn't think so.

But he was explaining; trying to make himself clear; it was not an autobiography: it was preparation for some point he had yet to make.

So this is early on, when utility companies and soft drink bottling companies and small local department stores aren't worried about what they've got in those computer files.

Well, they should be.

Because Arren Company is one of the early smugglers of data.

From the beginning of computers, there are crooks, and Arren Company is among them. Of course they don't consider themselves bad guys. They are just "availing themselves of data."

That summer, my brother turned seventeen, and a month later, I turned sixteen. Nobody was ever so happy to turn sixteen. I could buy my car and I could drive it away. My first car was a tiny little old Triumph, in terrible condition. (It is extra easy to get a Triumph into terrible condition.) I did bodywork, getting the dents out; I reupholstered the driver's seat. I had a lot of help. I suppose it's possible I was actually the helper. But I don't remember it that way. What I do remember was that the dealer took all my savings and then I had to sign a note promising to pay him another five hundred dollars. Back then? Serious money. Big bucks. It would take me forever.

Then suddenly my brother Rob was the one with big bucks. Lots of money. He didn't buy a fabulous car with it, which was what a normal person would do; he didn't even buy computers, which was what a weird person would do. He just stared at the money, as if it bothered him. How could extra money ever bother a person?

One day I was zipping him around in my Triumph, honking at everybody we knew and everybody we didn't, and he said, "Marc!" in a high, scared voice. I stared at him. Rob was sick-looking. Like he was going to throw up. "Don't get sick in my car," I warned him. I really cared about the upholstery and the carpeting. After all, I had installed them.

My brother gave me a blurry smile, a smile for things gone wrong, a smile for disaster. He put his hand on mine. We never touched. I don't remember ever giving my brother a hug. His hand on mine was startling.

Alice was appalled. She had no sister or brother to hug or not to hug. But she and Dad always greeted each other with hugs. She and Mom still cuddled.

Never touched your brother?

It seemed such a loss, such a terrible failure.

Alice wept.

Here, in this silent place — an apartment complex designed for people whose marriages died — her father really had died. He was gone. She had nothing left of him but the clothes in the closet and the journal on the disk.

The apartment was full and thick with nobody. Being alone was crushing Alice.

"What's the matter, Robbie?" I asked. I never called him Robbie. Not since we were really little, five and six.

"We're doing stuff we shouldn't be do-

ing," said my brother. I realized that he was thin, he'd lost weight, had developed a nervous habit of stroking his upper lip with his thumbnail.

"Marc," said my brother, "I'm the one doing it."

Rob and I were brought up with lots of talk about right and wrong. Our parents discussed it often. What other people did, what countries did, what presidents did, what we did. Right and wrong.

I never paid attention.

I mainly thought about cars and wrestling and boxing and baseball, though in the last year I'd been giving serious thought to girls and had actually started to spend money on something other than cars. Dates. I was beginning to wonder if maybe girls were better than cars.

So far the balance was in favor of cars.

"My after-school job is not helping Arren Company set up a payroll for a client," said Rob. "My after-school job is getting classified information from those companies while Dick Arren keeps them confused and occupied," said Rob.

I burst out laughing. "Twin," I said, "do you mean you are stealing?"

"We don't use the word steal," said Rob. "Dick Arren calls it spying, which is less guilty-sounding."

"Spy is a cool word," I agreed. "But I thought you were out at the hair dye place." The biggest employer in our city made shampoo and hand lotion and hair dyes and tints. It was impossible to imagine spies hanging out among bottles of goo.

"I am. Dick Arren is selling their formula to their competition. I'm the one getting the formulas."

At that moment, I was driving past the library. Two girls in Rob's class walked out. Karen and Donna had long thin straight hair and long curvy bodies. When they giggled and poked one another, their ribbons of hair seemed to blend and fold, and I fell in love. I honked. Karen and Donna, who probably never noticed Rob or me, did notice my car.

They grinned and waved.

Rob did not see them.

I decided on Karen. I was picturing Karen sitting where my brother was, while my brother was telling me about how when Dick Arren was working on payroll problems, they were problems Rob himself had set up. Dick Arren would joke with the secretaries and josh with the middle managers, while thin spotty-faced Rob would scour out the secrets which were hardly hidden at all but felt hidden to the company, because back then they didn't know that anybody passing through the system could pick up data and carry it away.

I drove on. Karen and Donna and the library vanished behind us.

"Who do I tell, Marc?" said my brother. "The police? The only police I know are guys who set up roadblocks on prom night to catch drinkers. They're not going to know from computers. Mom and Dad? The only parents I know are very heavily into right and wrong."

I could not work up the slightest interest in payrolls or hair dye. "Can't you just tell the shampoo company?"

"I'm a high school kid. I've never even met anybody there. Who would I talk to? Dick Arren smuggles me in and I pound away on the keyboard and I slip back out. Besides, Dick Arren is — well — he's not a normal guy, Marc."

I grinned. "I guess not. Your normal computer spy expert would at least be stealing from the Pentagon."

"I'm serious, Marc. He's not normal. There's something really off about Dick Arren."

"Why don't you just stop doing it then?" I said. I guess I was thinking of Rob's difficulty as a car. Trade it in. Give it a fresh coat of paint. Then sell it.

"Drop me off here," said Rob, and I dropped him off there.

Where was it?

I can tell you the corner. It was an intersection that doesn't mean a thing to me. Didn't then. Doesn't now.

Did my Twin, my only brother, just need to get out of the car? Was I failing him and he needed fresh air, and it wasn't me?

Or did he see something? Know something? Suddenly understand something? Did somebody live near there, or work near there, and he wanted to talk to them?

I never found out.

He got out, I yelled, "See you later," and I drove away, with no thoughts in my mind but Karen and Donna. A McDonald's had just been built near the library.

McDonald's wasn't common yet, and you were still thrilled at going into a store and getting a paper bag filled with burgers and fries. I cruised past McDonald's, but nobody I knew was there. I finally headed home.

Rob never came home.

He was killed that night.

Run over by a car out at the reservoir.

The reservoir was forbidden to the public. It was surrounded by a chain-link fence. Teenagers climbed over it, found the gravel road used by the water company, and walked in the dark to the water's edge.

But the night Rob died was a school night. Rob was the least likely person to go there. He never spent time out-of-doors; his life was in front of a screen. He had no car. The reservoir was miles from where I'd dropped him off.

The padlock on the water company's gate had been snapped. Half a mile down the lane, deep in the woods, Rob had been run over.

I went there later. There was no way to get hit by a car in the place where Rob got hit by a car. The road is very narrow, very curved. A car couldn't get up any speed.

Its headlights would be visible through the bare trees. If Rob had been standing in the road, he'd have taken a step back and put a tree trunk between himself and the car.

But Rob's body was found lying flat on the road. Not as if he'd been knocked down and then run over, but as if he'd been lying down already, and gotten run over.

Alcohol, said everybody, when they found Rob's body. Kids drinking. Remember how the same thing happened last year? Same spot? Very similar accident. Boys will be boys, they drink, they get stupid.

But there was no alcohol in Rob's blood.

Still, said everybody, it was kids, horsing around, not knowing when to stop.

But if it was kids, it wasn't kids from our high school, because we would have known. You always know that kind of stuff: who vandalized the school buses, who put firecrackers in the girls' locker room. Because that's why people do that stuff — so everybody else will know.

Nobody at our high school ran over my brother's body.

I told everybody what Rob had said to me in the car. The stealing of secrets from clients' data bases. "My brother died and it was no accident," I said over and over. "It was murder. Had to be. Dick Arren killed Rob because he was going to tell."

Our parents were furious with me. Bad enough they had lost their beloved older son — now I was trashing his good name? Calling him a thief about to confess?

Rob's math teacher (nobody taught computers yet) was scornful. Rob was a child; he did not have the computer skills or the chemistry knowledge to be obtaining secret formulas. I had been watching too much television.

The police were more courteous. They listened. They took notes. They questioned Mr. Arren. The man was shocked that I would say such things. And whatever he said to the police, it was good enough for them.

Nobody believed me.

Alice got up and took aspirin after all.

Her father's writing had gotten jumpy, changing tense and narrator, little short sentences and long run-on sentences. Her mind felt the same. Jumpy and changing and skidding on toward punctuation.

Two brothers murdered?

Could the two deaths be linked?

Could the same person have done each one? That would mean that Dad was killed by Dick Arren.

But had Uncle Rob been murdered? The police seemed to feel it was a terrible teenager accident, not a planned murder.

Besides... shampoo formula? It didn't seem important enough. Would you kill a boy because he was going to talk about shampoo formula?

The aloneness of the condo filled Alice, until her head swelled and her ears popped. She was thick with aloneness.

Dick Arren was a young man. People in computers were always young then. He was only in his twenties. Exactly ten years older than I am. He'd be forty-nine now. He was an attractive man, with fine blue eyes and fine thin features. There was something both elegant and hard about him.

He drove a black Porsche. I was awe-struck by that Porsche. A car to die for, I thought.

But the police told me that it was not the

car that killed Rob, and I had to believe that. I said to the police: A person can own two cars. He can rent a car, borrow a car, steal a car. It was Dick Arren, I know it was!

Cool off, son, said the police.

After school, after the funeral, I drove to the offices where Dick Arren's Porsche was parked, and when he left work, I followed him, he in his Porsche and me in my Triumph. He'd stop at a red light and I'd pull up next to him, driving right up on the sidewalk if I had to, and I'd yell, "I know what you did, and I'm going to prove it!"

Arren grinned, and took off way faster than I could, and we were in a weird sick drag race that I could only lose.

He should have been afraid of me. Even at sixteen, I was bigger than Dick Arren. I was bigger than most people. But he was not afraid. A man who has killed another man knows he can do something extraordinary: He can take a life.

But he was not afraid of me. He was enjoying himself. He let me catch him. This time I pulled up next to Arren and he waved a wooden pencil — a yellow Ticonderoga pencil — out of his window and twirled it baton-style in his fingers. Then, smiling — a wide delighted ultrahappy smile; the smile, indeed, of a man who was not normal — he snapped the pencil in half. The pieces dropped onto the pavement between us. He giggled. "That's your brother, kid," he said. "Garbage in the road." He gunned the Porsche and left me behind.

I wanted to grab Dick Arren by the hair and jerk his head back, breaking his neck. The sound of his spine cracking would be music to my ears.

But I could not chase him once he decided to use that Porsche the way it was designed to be driven, and I could not find him again, not at home, not at his office, not anywhere, so I went to the police.

But of course Dick Arren denied to the police and my parents that he had said any such thing. He told my parents sympathetically that he would be happy to help pay for psychiatric help for me. My parents liked him. They thought he was a fine fellow. They didn't think much of me, harassing and threatening an innocent man.

And soon after this, there was nobody to follow. The company was gone. The office was empty. The house was empty. The garage was empty. The phone was disconnected.

Arren had bailed out.

I went to the police again, and they said, "He can run a computer business from anywhere. Why should he stay here and put up with you?"

My parents didn't live long after that. My dad had a heart attack when I was twenty and didn't recover. Mom was lonely, with me at college and no husband at home. I've always thought she mentally lay down in the road, like the son she missed so badly, and let her physical problems run over her.

I was an orphan at twenty-two, and there was no big brother to be Twins with. I found a job with a computer company myself and began to cast my computer net to find Dick Arren. I'd make him lie down in the road.

I embarked on a newspaper search, which covered many cities and many years. I was going to find Dick Arren.

And then something happened to change my life utterly and forever. I met a beautiful wonderful girl named Chrissie.

Chrissie made me a better person. Together we created a perfect daughter. That baby was the love of my life. I would come home from work laughing, just thinking how my baby Alice would throw herself on top of me, shouting, "Daddy!" I never knew what a great word that was — Daddy! — until I heard it from my own child.

But my need for revenge never lessened. It was deep within me, sometimes all over and through me.

No wonder Dad liked a car called Avenger.

No wonder Dad played Escape and Chase. He'd been chasing for twenty-three years.

Alice did not know which was more awful: the idea of a killer whose viciousness had touched her own family, or the idea of Dad chasing him for so many years. Dad had not taken all those new jobs because of the money or the excitement of the work — he'd been trying to get closer to Dick Arren. The tragedy of Rob's death had become an obsession.

Oh, Dad, why didn't you tell us! Did you

think I was too little? For ten or twelve years, you were right. But I'm fifteen now, Dad. You could have included me.

"I would have understood, Daddy," Alice whispered, and then she thought: *but Mom wouldn't have.* She'd never have let Dad dedicate his life to revenge. Living is better. Laughing and loving is better.

So. Was Dick Arren out there, using another name? Still in computers? Still stealing formulas?

Who did Alice know, age fifty? Elegant and hard and blue-eyed and a computer expert? A man in his twenties who drove a Porsche would drive something spectacular in his fifties, too.

Mr. Scote and Mr. Austin were middle-aged and drove great cars. Mr. Scote had a silver Jag; Mr. Austin, a Mercedes. They were certainly into computers.

And yet — a Lumina minivan was in this. A Lumina was an unpopular, unsuccessful, low-end model. Did a former Porsche owner pick out a Lumina?

Had Dad, like Rob, been murdered by his employer? Was Mr. Scote or Mr. Austin really Dick Arren? But why on earth would Dad voluntarily go to work for Dick

Arren? Surely her father could not have stayed sane, showing up for work every day with the man he believed had snapped Rob in two.

And if Dad had finally located Dick Arren, and that was what this disk was about, why hadn't Dad been ready when the bad guys came? Dad was big and strong and full of fight. He'd planned for years. He knew the enemy was dangerous. *Why hadn't he been ready?*

"Oh, Daddy!" she cried, and she had to get away from the gray and careless screen. She tottered in the dark to the small living room and fell to her knees and curled over the coffee table, clinging to its sides, wanting things to be different.

The phone rang.

The sound of the bell burst through her head and she convulsed on the carpet, almost yanking the table over. Could she live through the sound of her father's cheerful voice explaining that neither he nor Alice could come to the phone right now?

But the answering machine did not pick up.

It had been the fax.

Alice listened to the harsh cry of the machine and the sound of a single page inching out.

She had to crawl back to the desk and drag herself up by the knobs on the drawers and reach for the page. She stumbled into the bathroom to turn on the light and read the fax.

It was from James.

Marc — What are you waiting for? I've tried E-mail, I've tried phone, I'm down to fax. Now send the stuff so I can download. Condense to one page. Nobody's going to read more than that.

Too bad the only photograph of Dick Arren is twenty-five years old. We should hire somebody to do a computer aging process, guess at what he'd look like now. As soon as you send me the WANTED poster, we'll get it out on the Internet.

Dad had planned to put the story of Rob's death on the Internet. He was through asking around locally. He was going to ask globally.

Dad must have been ready to send his WANTED poster when the killer walked in on him.

The events of that terrible day were becoming clear now.

Dad realized he was in trouble, but not how much trouble. He'd called Alice to get the disks, and he didn't want anybody to know where she was going with them.

Then he ran out of time.

He had not found the killer. The killer had found him. Right up to the end, they had been drag racing, and the killer's car was still faster.

Alice could take no more.

She made it to the couch. She felt her headache fall off, sliding down into sleep, and she slid with it.

Chapter 11

Alice snapped awake.

Somebody was cranking a stalled engine.

Daylight made pale rims around the pleated blinds in the living room windows.

Two other cars started up, decently and quietly. People were leaving for work.

Alice had planned to get out of Dad's condo when it was still dark; when no alarm clock had gone off, no automatic coffeemaker had begun to drip in a dark kitchen, no neighbors were turning the keys in their locks, glancing around and seeing Alice. Now she would have to leave in daylight.

She had had plans for the day: clear, careful, intelligent plans. But she could not bring them to mind. Okay, she said to herself. Okay.

She was like a kindergarten teacher, trying to coax all her little thoughts to get in line.

Last night I realized that Dad and his friend James believe there is a killer out there. A killer who has been around twenty-five years. If Dad was murdered by this person, he's still out there, ready to do it again. A killer whose voice I heard: *I killed him good.* As Rob had said, not normal.

Last night Alice had stripped off the clothing stolen from Amanda but had not changed out of her jeans and T-shirt from the mall. It was strange to sleep in her clothes, even stranger to be filthy and not care. She looked like what she was: a girl on the run. Alice yanked her hair into a ponytail to help herself think.

What would the former Dick Arren be doing right now? He had killed another person, and surely it was time to abandon this place and this identity. No doubt he was packing. Throwing files and papers into boxes, cramming suitcases full, calling the airlines. Perhaps he already had a new identity and a place to go. Perhaps, while she slept, he had already vanished. If Alice did not take action today, he'd be gone, and history would repeat itself.

You will not get away with murder this time, she thought. Not Rob's and not Dad's. You will not laugh from the safety of another name and another city. I will move too fast for you.

Last night she'd half thought that Dick Arren must now be Mr. Scote or Mr. Austin. This morning that conclusion seemed flimsy. After all, Dick Arren would recognize Dad's name. He would not hire Marc Robie, because he'd remember Marc Robie as vividly as Marc Robie remembered him. She was basing her conclusion solely on the fact that Mr. Scote and Mr. Austin were middle-aged and drove great cars.

Her stomach hurt from emptiness and yet the thought of food was nauseating. She did not even want to go near the refrigerator for orange juice. It was too normal. People with ordinary lives, calm lives, lives that worked out — those people had a glass of orange juice in the morning.

Alice could only stand in the half light and have half thoughts.

The file called TWIN was not the sort of

thing that would become a wanted poster for the Internet. It was long, and rambling, and full of personal detail that nobody but Dad, or Alice, would care about. Perhaps, she thought, it was just for him. He was sorting out the worst subject of his life. Getting ready to choose the dozen sentences he'd actually use on the wanted poster. Or perhaps there's another file, accessible by a password I don't know. Perhaps somewhere, a twenty-five-year-old photograph of Dick Arren.

It was way beyond Alice's capacity to sort this out.

Only the authorities had the time and expertise to follow Dad's years of research and locate the real Dick Arren.

The awful time had come in which she was going to have to turn herself in. There would be a period in which nobody believed her. She would have to accept that. Everybody, including her mother, had accepted the E-mail confession.

Alice would have to face people who were horrified by her, who would treat her as a vicious animal, and she would have to stay calm and convince them that yes, there was a vicious animal out there, and it was a man formerly known as Dick Arren.

She could do this with her mother at her side.

Of course ... *Mom might not be at her side.*

She said she was, Alice told herself. Mom said she loved me no matter what I did. I have to count on that. I can go home.

She imagined Mom forcing herself to touch her daughter, flinching because they were related, sick because she was picturing Alice hitting Dad.

I have to be brave enough to get through that, Alice told herself. I have to believe Mom will believe me later.

And what if I'm wrong? What if nobody does believe me ever? What if nobody can find Dick Arren, if nobody tries to look — because nobody thinks there's a reason to?

Alice had no choice. The situation was too large and terrible for her to go on alone.

She had no friends to call upon. Her classmates had gone after her as if she were a fish in tournament. They were wading around in their hip boots, sweeping their nets, eager to catch Alice.

She considered calling the police from

here. But what if they came and did not let her see her mother? What if it was like some Monopoly game card — Go straight to Jail? No. She had to go home, and once she was with Mom, whatever happened would happen.

Wait.

There was one person who would believe her. James.

Alice stumbled around the condo, trying to find the fax. She was so muddled that she could hardly tell what was paper, what was book, what was plastic. There it was. Lying on Dad's desk. Alice snatched it up, and sure enough, the heading on the fax gave James's last name.

Alice turned on the computer, grateful that she used it so much that the movements were automatic for her; making her way through each command did not require thought. She went into Dad's address book. There was the E-mail address for James. Alice opened the document and sent him the entire TWIN file.

She found herself playing with the computer, wanting to hang out and search for the stored photo and the wanted poster. She went back to Dad's address book and read through names. Who else should I send TWIN to?

I'm killing time, she thought. I'm afraid to leave the condo. I'm so scared of what's going to happen next.

She made herself leave the computer, but it didn't get her out the door. She wandered around. She would drive the Blazer, which had extra power outlets. With phone and laptop, Alice would have a command center. From her bedroom, Alice got her laptop. In the kitchen, she got the spare keys to Dad's Blazer.

She stared into the garage, her feet exactly where her father's killer's had been. If her guesses were right, Dick Arren had stood here. Was he Austin? Scote? Another employee? A client? Or was he a neighbor right here in Stratford Condominiums?

The people in the next condo would be shaken when they heard a car start from the empty home of a murdered man. She had to move fast. Alice had no fast left in her. She had only slow and muddled. She forced herself to climb behind the wheel of the Blazer. *What if her very own mother was afraid of her?*

Alice turned the key; the engine caught; she hit the garage door remote and backed out.

Even at this hour, the roads were crowded and slow. No matter how early you got started, so did everybody else. Alice headed through the city to her mother's house. Her hands were puffy with heat and fear. It was hard to hold the steering wheel.

Traffic was useful. Because she had to think about it, it kept her busy and anxious. But once she crossed the center of town and began to head back toward the suburbs again, traffic was light. Nobody drove in this direction in the morning.

Alice gave calming orders to her body, but her body refused them and became hotter, more tense. Explosions were building inside her, and she must not let this happen; she must be rational and careful.

She turned the last corner. Tree branches hung too low, and houses she had known for years were hunched and dark. She felt spied upon, expected. Neighbors who had once been her friends were peeking behind curtains, whispering to each other — There she is! She's giving up!

I am not giving up, thought Alice. I have plenty of fight left in me.

She swung into her mother's driveway. She drove all the way around the house and parked in back, hidden from prying eyes by a low hill covered with swooping shrubs. The garage doors were open. Mom's good car was not there.

Alice stared at the garage.

Mom wasn't home?

Impossible!

She had to be home.

And there were no other cars, either. No police, no friends, no nothing.

Alice had no key, and Mom didn't keep a spare outside. Alice left the Blazer idling and ran to the back door, knocking, and then hammering, and then shouting, "Mom!"

It was Friday. A workday. But even if Mom left this early for work — which she didn't — she wouldn't go to work when she was waiting for Alice to call, would she?

She stayed at Richard Rellen's, thought Alice.

Alice forgot everything. How dare she! Maybe Mom didn't even mind that this was happening. Maybe it was a nice chance to be in Richard Rellen's arms. Maybe Mom was so drunk with love that this was an opportunity for her.

Would Mom sacrifice Alice to her own second chance at love?

Parents did it all the time.

How many families did Alice know of where divorce ripped them apart once, and remarriage ripped them apart a second time? How many kids did Alice know who were going to college solely to escape a parent's remarriage? Or worse, to escape the endless dating of a parent, the leaping from one boyfriend to another, the broken hearts, the teenager having to be parent to the parent?

Why hadn't the police staked out the house, the way they did on television, ready to seize Alice? Perhaps in real life there weren't enough police to go around, or perhaps they believed Alice long gone. Out of state by now.

Alice got back in the Blazer. She didn't back up but circled hard and fast over Mom's precious grass, wishing she could leave tracks like that on Mom's heart.

She drove to Richard Rellen's, going faster and seeing less.

His house was large, and its four-car garage faced sideways, so that from the street, it was just two quaint windows and a cupola. He had a lot of yard help, and the landscaping was flawless, every flag-stone neatly edged, every flower carefully mulched.

She'd been in his house once. Mom stopped by to bring Rick darling some dessert she had baked — yes, Mom was that woozy about the man, baking little treats for him! Alice had refused to go in and sat in the car. After half an hour, Mom and Mr. Rellen had come out and said they had ordered pizza, come on in and share with us, and Alice had broken down, gone in and shared with them. She never told Dad.

Alice swung into the long split driveway, expecting to see her mother's car. It was not visible. Well, at least Mom felt guilty enough that she'd driven into the garage to hide her presence from the neighbors.

Most people Alice knew had lots of cars. The parents each had one, and there'd be one for each teenager, maybe one for haul-ing, possibly one for showing off.

The garages were closed, but a row of windows ran across the big doors.

The Blazer was relatively high. Craning her neck, she could glimpse what was parked inside.

A big power boat occupied the first slot. Alice had not known about the boat. Did Rick darling and Mom go to the lake in that boat?

In the second was the green Volvo wagon. Rick darling was home anyway.

In the third was a beautiful classic Porsche, probably thirty years old, an incredibly lovely car; a collector's joy.

The fourth was not visible. The windows were blocked with paper that had faded. How tacky and sloppy it looked above the neatly swept driveway.

The Blazer's engine chugged on. Alice sat with her foot on the brake and her mind in neutral.

A heavy hand closed on the door handle, and ripped it open, yanking Alice out before she could think, before she could struggle. Richard Rellen held her arm, and incredibly, he was smiling.

The Blazer was still in gear, and it moved forward by itself. It had little time to gather speed, but it was heavy, and the garage door nothing but pressboard, and the Blazer slammed right through the fourth door and into whatever was parked there. The all-too-distinctive sound of crunching metal filled the morning air. The windows broke and fell in that strange, straight-down collapse of safety glass, a million teeny, harmless squares coming down on the hood of the Blazer.

"You didn't have to do that," said Alice. Her reserve strength vanished and she began sobbing. She tried to free herself from his grip, but he was way too strong. She stopped. After all, she wasn't going anywhere. "I was coming to turn myself in. Now I've dented both cars, and Mom will be even madder."

"I don't think she cares about the cars," said Mr. Rellen. "Let's go inside, Alice."

"Is Mom there?"

"No. Your mother has gone to the airport to meet your grandparents. She'll be back in an hour."

"Oh," said Alice. She felt stupid and young. Mom was not somewhere being wrong or evil. Just going to the airport to get her own mother and father. Grandma and Grandpa were coming to the rescue.

Her grandparents thought Alice was

perfect. They told her so all the time. They would be on her side. They would listen, and love, and agree. Alice's tears became relief; family was coming, people who loved her.

Mr. Rellen moved her toward the house, in a practiced, steady way; the way Paul of the computer lab had escorted her.

Alice said, "But if Mom drove to the airport, what car is in the fourth space?"

Mr. Rellen smiled even more broadly. The smile decorated his face like a spaceship: an alien object that had no business being there. *Spaceship.* Alice swerved and looked back, and through the broken windows, lit by the rising sun, she could see the unmistakable spaceship front end of a navy blue Lumina minivan.

Mr. Rellen was chuckling. Alice stared at him. She stared at where his strong thick fingers held her own arm.

How close the name Rick Rellen was to the name Dick Arren.

The best disguise is weight. Richard Rellen was heavy. If he had an elegant jaw, it was now obscured by a beard.

Could Alice's mother actually be in love with the killer of Alice's father? What a last laugh for Dick Arren — ending the life and taking the wife of his pursuer.

Alice's mind sealed over at the idea of having eaten pizza and sat on the couch with that human being. "You killed my father," she whispered. "You killed his brother, too! *Where is my mother? Have you killed her?*"

He said nothing but kept walking toward the house, and Alice had no hope of freeing herself. She stopped walking and let herself drop, a deadweight, the way strikers did when police tried to arrest them, but it did not work for Alice; Richard Rellen just picked her up.

I'm just like Dad, thought Alice, stunned. I knew there was a bad guy. Why hadn't I been ready? . . .

"Is that the same Porsche?" said Alice. "Is that the car you drove when Rob drove his Triumph?"

"What can you be talking about, Alice?" asked Richard Rellen, smiling again.

"That's why you didn't yell and run after me and call the police when you caught me on campus. You had my backpack, and you knew Dad's disks had to be in it."

They were almost at the door. She could

not let him take her inside. Inside, because nobody knew she was here, would be just as remote as a reservoir. She could see no point in screaming: people never looked up for annoyances like that — car alarms rang till they died and nobody went over to see why. If Alice screamed, he would put his hand over her mouth and suffocate her.

"It won't work," she said. "I have an E-mail master list on my laptop. I sent everybody the wanted poster with the updated photograph of you. So you can kill me, but you can't do it in secret. I've notified the world."

Rellen's smile vanished.

Without a smile, the face seemed to belong to different people. Several of them.

Then he laughed. "There is no updated photograph, Alice. Because if there were, you'd have recognized me. You wouldn't have come here, would you?" He reached for the door. The house had a decorative screen door and a heavy wooden storm door behind it. Both were closed. He was going to need a hand free to open them. Alice did not bother trying to free herself. She tried to keep his other hand occupied instead. She grabbed it and bit it and braced her flimsy torn sneakers against the door jamb.

He enjoyed it. Was that the last thing poor Uncle Rob had seen before his death? And Dad? Had he seen? At the last minute, facing the man his wife meant to marry, had he realized the terrible awful coincidence of this? Had Dad heard this sick chuckle, looked into this sick smile?

Maybe it was not a coincidence. Maybe Mr. Rellen purposely found Mom and got a laugh out of being Mr. Perfect to the woman whose husband was trying to hunt him down.

Alice heard a siren. Then two. Was there a car accident? Was there a fire? Or was this the sound of rescue?

Alice scratched him with the long hard false fingernails, making bloody tracks on his ugly fat hairy arm. He shoved her against the house wall and held her with his chest while he opened the screen door and the storm door.

A car drove into Rellen's driveway.

Two cars. Three. Four.

Police.

Horns honked. Doors slammed. Feet pounded.

Richard Rellen released her and Alice slipped to the ground. So many people! Police in uniform, men and women not in uniform, people with guns in their hands. The guns were *out*, were *drawn*.

"Be very careful," said Richard Rellen calmly. "She's truly violent." He held up his bleeding arm. "She may be on crack. Or some hallucinogenic drug. There's more here than just an emotional teenage girl."

One officer said, "If you'd step away from Alice, sir . . ."

"Of course. Please think of Alice's mother first. She's a fragile woman who has suffered many shocks. For her sake, be gentle with Alice."

"We'll do that, sir," said the officer. He put his gun away.

Alice pressed her back against the house, terrified of them all.

Mr. Rellen said, "She was crazed when she got here. She drove her father's car right through the garage, screaming things about her mother." He pointed. The Blazer's engine was still running, trying to drive on through the building. It was an eerie sight. "Very sad," said Mr. Rellen.

"Poor Chrissie. She hasn't done anything to deserve this."

He's used to bluffing, thought Alice. After all, he's been doing it successfully for a quarter of a century. And now I know how easy a bluff is, how well it works. You walk into the dorm, you steal a car, you use an elementary school, you fib in the bagel line — all you have to do is stay calmer than the people around you and they don't question you any longer.

He'll win, she thought dizzily. I've had two days of practice and he's had twenty-five years, and he'll win.

An officer stood on each side of her, lifted Alice, and walked her toward a police car. She could not speak to defend herself. She was completely overwhelmed with the numbers against her.

"It's over, Alice," said the officer. "Let's go sit in my car."

They slid into the front seat: one officer behind the wheel, Alice in the middle, the other policeman at the door. She was surprised in an exhausted blurry way: Didn't prisoners sit in the back behind the grill?

"You're okay, Alice," said the officer gently. "You were a brave girl. Dumb, but brave. Your father's colleagues got in touch with us the minute they realized he'd been murdered. It can't be the daughter, they said, it's got to be the killer he's been hunting. We let it stay on the news that we suspected you because we didn't want the killer to vanish. We didn't know about Richard Rellen. When your mother mentioned him, we put him on our list to talk to, but we had a bunch of names ahead of his. We figured with your mother dating him, your father would have met him and recognized him right away, no matter what amount of weight or hair or beard had changed. But in fact, your father never laid eyes on Richard Rellen."

"You don't think it's me?" said Alice. "You know he sent the E-mail confession? My mother isn't afraid of me?"

"Your mother is afraid *for* you, Alice. She hasn't slept or moved from the telephone since this began."

Fears ran off Alice like water from the shower. She felt cleaner and clearer. Mom still loved her.

"How did you find me?"

"Your high school friends. They couldn't believe you had hurt your father. They believed you were a hostage, and somebody hidden in the backseat of all those cars was forcing you to drive away." He grinned. "Though when you ran away from the boys in the Jeep, that theory got shaken up."

"It was awful," said Alice. "They stalked me. They wanted to throw me to the ground."

"I don't think so. I think they wanted to help. We tried to stop them and make them go to school, but you actually had a lot of admirers who weren't going to listen to any crap about how you hurt anybody. So they were out there in the roads, trying to find you and help. A girlfriend of yours was up at dawn. Kelsey was sure you'd go home. She said your whole life was home. She saw you drive away from your mother's house and she followed you here. Kelsey called in from her car phone."

Alice was so tired she could not even picture her best friend. She could think only of being with her mother again. "Are you arresting Mr. Rellen?"

"We're reading him his rights and asking

him to come down to headquarters to talk. You just sit here between us and don't look. It isn't pretty."

"*I'm* not pretty. I'm filthy and disgusting."

"Yeah, but you're alive. That's pretty cool. You know, Alice, if you had just trusted one grown-up, if you'd called just one friend, we would have reached you and explained what we knew and you wouldn't have had to go through this."

"I did call!" she said. "I called home. The policewoman sure didn't make it sound like she believed in me."

"Nobody handled this real well," he admitted. "We don't have many murders like this. We were all a little crazed the first day. Just like you. And it was a heck of a confession, Alice. Everybody fell for it at first." He paused. "Where did you spend the nights?"

"A girl at State University let me stay in her room. She didn't call you?"

"Nobody called us."

So Ginger just thought Alice was an incredibly rude houseguest who fled in the morning without saying thank you. And perhaps Amanda, with her large wardrobe, had not noticed anything missing. And maybe Paul, with exams on his mind, had not thought of her again.

Alice said, "I want my mother." Alice whimpered softly.

He nodded. "Hop in the backseat; I can't drive around with you up front. We'll go over to your house. Your mom and your grandparents should be back from the airport. You just hang on another ten minutes."

"Does she know yet about Richard Rellen?"

"No."

"Maybe she'll be on his side."

"She'll be on your side. You're her world, Alice. And we've known for twenty-four hours that your father was not killed in the condo, but brought there dead, so you couldn't have done it."

"Where was he killed?"

"We don't know yet. Maybe Mr. Rellen will tell us. Maybe a quick look at his home and office will tell us."

Alice got in the back. Like Bethany's van, it had old and unpleasant smells. Like Bethany's van, it was a rest from running.

I'm safe. Mom loves me. I still have a

home. I had friends all along. But I don't have Daddy.

She said to her father: I did my best. I'm sorry I didn't do better. I was pretty dumb most of the time. But so were you! Oh, Daddy, why weren't you ready? Why didn't you win?

"Here we are," said the officer, "and there's your mom."

They had to let her out of the car. The doors didn't open from the inside. By the time Alice was out, her mother was on top of her, and they were sobbing and hugging, and her grandmother was saying, "That girl needs a bath!" and her grandfather was saying, "Alice, Alice."

And Alice was saying over and over the most important word left to her: "Mom!"

About the Author

Caroline B. Cooney lives in a small seacoast village in Connecticut. She writes every day on a word processor and then goes for a long walk down the beach to figure out what she's going to write the following day. She's written over fifty books for young people, including, *The Party's Over*, *The Face on the Milk Carton Trilogy*, *Flight #116 Is Down*, *Flash Fire*, *Emergency Room*, *The Stranger*, and *Twins*.

Ms. Cooney reads as much as possible, and has three grown children.

CAROLINE B. COONEY

Caroline B. Cooney—Takes You To The Edge Of Your Seat!

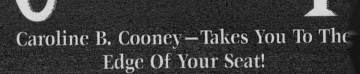

BCE98849-2	**Wanted!**	$4.50
BCE45680-6	**The Stranger**	$4.50
BCE45740-3	**Emergency Room**	$4.50
BCE44479-4	**Flight #116 Is Down**	$4.50
BCE47478-2	**Twins**	$4.50

Available wherever you buy books, or use this order form.

THRILLERS